TRACE EVIDENCE

TRACE EVIDENCE

A KATE CARPENTER THRILLER

VANESSA ROBERTSON

WILD JUSTICE PRESS

ISBN: 9781916009813

Published by Wild Justice Press

For Mum - thanks for buying me my first typewriter

PROLOGUE

The Labrador ran along the ridge, casting about, before picking up a scent in the air. Pausing, he looked towards his owner, still climbing up the flank of the hill. Lifting his nose again, curious and questing, he ran a little further, darting between rocks. The man called to him with a hint of irritation in his voice. He was ready to turn for home and rain clouds were scudding in from the west. The dog reappeared with something in his mouth and cantered back to his master, dropping the object at his feet and waiting for praise.

Bending, curious, the man picked up the empty plastic pill container and looked at the label. A medication with a long name that meant nothing to him but it was an odd thing to find discarded up here in the hills. They were well off the usual path taken by walkers, rarely seeing another soul along this barely-used sheep track.

The dog ran off again, keen and purposeful, and his owner, still turning the pill bottle in his hand, called him back. He was rewarded with a flick of the dog's ear—he was listening but he'd obey when he was ready. For now, he was on a mission.

Appearing from between the rocks, the dog had something else in his mouth this time. He scampered back, ready to listen to his master's commands now. The man bent and took hold of the object and the dog pulled, teeth tightened, wanting to turn this into a game of tug. A sharp word and he gave up the woollen hat, a little snagged now from his teeth. A hat and an empty pill bottle.

The dog turned again, set to return to the rocks and his owner reached for him quickly, snapping on his lead. Pulling towards the rocks, intent on whatever he'd found there, the dog's curiosity piqued the man's and he let the dog tow him towards the outcrop. He rounded the largest rock and discovered, if not an actual cave, a hollow space that must have sheltered many sheep from wind and rain over the centuries.

But not today. At that moment, it was sheltering a body, clad in walking gear and accompanied by more pill packets and an empty whisky bottle.

Pulling the dog's lead, backing away towards fresh air as he fumbled for his mobile phone, the dog walker swallowed down a rush of bile. The smell wasn't as bad out in the open, just a faint sweetness that caught in the back of the throat. But the man knew that this person was beyond his help, beyond anyone's help now. All he could do was alert the authorities and maintain a lonely vigil until they got there.

1

From the bushes, stock-still and on a hair-trigger to flee, the gazelles watched the first of our vehicles pass on the rough road. But the noise of the second SUV was too unsettling however and they pivoted and sprinted for cover, lithe, graceful, and fast as the wind.

I turned my head, trying to watch them a little longer, but they were gone and neither Pete nor the two former soldiers in the truck in front were slowing down to look at wildlife. We were here to do a job, not sight-see. If I wanted to do that I would have to come back another time. And with different companions.

It was getting on for eleven o'clock and hot, with temperatures expected to hit the forties later. Rolling my shoulders, already sticking to the seat, I cursed my bad luck at making this trip in an unexpected heatwave. Escaping the Scottish winter for a couple of days was one thing, but this was not the relaxing mini-break I'd have preferred. Still, another hour or so driving, collect the painting, then back to the hotel before flying home to the UK the next morning. I took a mouthful of water, tepid now, and passed the bottle to Pete.

"Thanks." It was the first time either of us had spoken in quite a while.

"S'okay." A vulture circled away to our left and I hoped it wasn't a bad omen. I massaged my wrist. The fracture had mended but it was sore from hefting my luggage the day before. However, the satisfaction of getting the better of the thug who'd attacked me had been worth it and it seemed a small price to pay for breaking his jaw.

"Wrist okay now?" Pete asked, glancing over.

"Mostly. I'll try to avoid thumping anyone else for a bit."

"You need to spend more time in the boxing gym. Improve your technique a bit."

"Probably." I smiled, looking out of the window. Pete was always practical.

"Did you sleep well last night?" He was clearly feeling more talkative now.

"Not really. It was too hot." Too hot and I'd been too aware of Pete in the next room, too aware of the tension between us earlier in the evening, too aware of the words unsaid. It was a couple of months since we'd last met and a lot had changed, but where to start?

"Nor me," he went on. "There was a fan but, you know, it didn't do much."

And we fell back into silence, seemingly accepting that we couldn't stretch out a conversation about the inadequacy of our hotel's ventilation and my lack of skill with a straight left any longer. So while the elephants in the room made themselves comfortable, I screwed the lid onto the water bottle and returned to gazing out of the window.

. . .

THE PAINTING we were in South Africa to recover was a small oil of a woman in a Parisian cafe by Pierre-Auguste Renoir, conservatively valued at a couple of million pounds. Probably less at the moment, as from the pictures I'd seen it seemed to have had a rough time of it over the last seventy years—taken off its wooden stretchers, rolled up, and mostly hidden away. Unloved and shabby now, but a good restorer would make it sing again.

It was a charming piece that had also pleased the eye of the German SS officer who'd appropriated it at the end of World War II when he left Berlin and fled to South Africa. There, the painting had allegedly remained in a cupboard while he lived out his life anonymously in a community where everyone, including his family, insisted that they were completely ignorant of his Nazi background.

The Renoir had passed through a couple of generations and only come to my attention when the grandson who'd inherited the painting, Julius Hoffman, made enquiries about selling it. Although it had been packed away for decades, he claimed that it was an original work and was looking for a price reflecting that. Apparently, it had been in the family since well before the war, bought in Paris way back in the 1920s. It wasn't a convincing story; there was no paperwork of any sort and no-one kept a genuine Renoir in their understairs cupboard if they came by it legitimately.

The auction house Hoffman took the artwork to became suspicious and had a quiet word with me and, armed with photographs, I'd tracked down the Renoir's rightful owners who'd long ago given up hope of ever seeing it again. I visited them in The Hague and their excitement that this painting, a talisman for their family since the horrors of the death camps, had resurfaced brought tears to my eyes. I might chase stolen artworks for the buzz and the hefty fees I charged, but the looted pieces I traced, charging nothing but expenses, were what I got the most satisfaction from.

Hoffman couldn't sell the work and having it seized by the authorities would begin a tortuous legal process so we decided that negotiation would be the best way forward. For over a year I'd been working on this, finally persuading the young man that despite his grandfather evading justice all his life, this was an important means to make amends, even if to a tiny degree, for what he'd been part of. It wouldn't change the past, but it would help towards healing wounds, and not only for the Larssen family.

With great diplomacy, I had cajoled and encouraged and charmed and finally, it had been arranged that I'd go to the family's farm in South Africa where the Renoir would be handed over and I would take it back to Europe to return it to the Larssens from whom it had been seized in the late thirties.

"So, how do you know Andy and Wally?" I asked as we drove on. I wasn't sure what Wally's real name was. I hoped it wasn't Wally.

"We go way back. Pre-Iraq even." Pete had suggested we take the two men in the other vehicle when, a little nervous after my run-in with Yuri Sokolov's not-so-tame heavies, I'd been wary about heading off to the heart of Africa.

"And what do they do now? Out here?"

"They work for a conservation charity. Tracking animals, pursuing poachers. That sort of thing." Pete's tone was casual, deceptively so I thought, and I suspected that they were up to a lot more. I couldn't see former Special Forces soldiers being happy to settle for a career patting hippos and the like.

"Lucky you had them to call on." I was struggling but determined to try and break the awkward silence. "I wasn't keen on the look of Hoffman when I checked out his social media. Too much posing with guns and proclaiming far-right attitudes for my liking."

"I noticed that too. Luckily Andy and Wally know the lie of the land and could get all the gear we needed. I wasn't risking turning up here without knowing that we could deal with anything young Hoffman tried. And it's good to catch up, I haven't seen them for a couple of years."

"So I gathered." Our companions seemed pleasant enough, but not chatty. Definitely the strong, silent, borderline psychopathic types. Given Pete's less than jolly mood, I'd gone to bed early the previous night, leaving the three of them in the bar reminiscing about the old days.

I was nervous about today's trip. Something felt a little off about Hoffman, beyond even the white supremacist stuff, and not knowing what was going to greet us at our destination, I was glad to have the three men with me, awkward tension and lack of social skills notwithstanding. Consequently, half an hour before we were due to arrive at the farm, we parked in the shade of some trees to put on body armour and unlock the gun cases secured in the backs of the Land Cruisers.

In my day job as art advisor to a number of wealthy individuals, I spent a lot of time in galleries and auction houses looking groomed and polished. Today was quite a contrast: faded Levis, hiking boots and a Kevlar vest, with my hair in a plait and a gun on my hip.

To be honest, the weapon was mainly a deterrent and very much a last resort; I was a lucky shot rather than a good one. As well as putting in some sessions at the boxing gym, Pete often pointed out that on my trips to the States I could benefit from some more coaching at a shooting range

. . .

We drove on, pausing at the farm gate to exchange looks and nods with the guys in the other truck, and then headed up to the house. It was a low wooden structure, comfortable rather than flashy, and a little shabby with some of the yellowing white paint flaking here and there.

It was uncannily quiet; no people, no vehicles, no dogs running out to greet us. While Pete and I waited, the other two men got out and knocked on the front door. No answer. Weapons drawn, they set off to circle the buildings. Pete looked thoughtful.

"What do you think?" I asked.

"Something doesn't feel right. This was the Nazi grandfather's place?"

"Yes. Hoffman said the family just use it as a holiday house now."

"And you called him yesterday?"

"I did. We've spoken three times this week and I rang him again last night, just to check that this was still the plan. He seemed okay. Not friendly, but I think he might simply have an unfortunate manner." I was unsettled and that feeling didn't ebb away when Andy and Wally reappeared, grim-faced. I wound down my window.

"No-one home."

"You're kidding me?" I got out of the Land Cruiser and looked around. "They've gone out?"

"Sorry Kate, they've left for good, I'd say. The house is stripped bare from what we saw through the windows. You need to see this too."

Andy nodded to the side of the house and we all trooped round. On the terrace at the back, next to a dried out and cracked swimming pool, four large stones weighted down the corners of a piece of canvas about three feet by two. I could see from the edges that it had once been a painting, but it was splashed with something, the centre completely eaten away. Heart racing, I squatted down to look more closely and instinctively reached out for it. Pete grabbed me before I could touch it.

"Don't. It's acid."

I bent lower, squinting in the strong sunlight, and I could see the chemical still burning its way through pigments and canvas. The little bastard. Rather than hand the painting over, Hoffman had destroyed it. And why? If he'd changed his mind about surrendering it, why not just keep it? What had meant so much to the Larssens, far more than its monetary value, had been discarded as nothing by him. And the artistic loss; I looked at the bubbling and fading paint applied by a genius almost a century and a half earlier and was hit by a wave of utter fury.

"How long's this been here?" I asked, looking around as if I expected to see Hoffman hiding behind a tree. "Not long, surely? It's still fizzing. He can't have got far."

"Far enough that we're probably not going to catch him. Do you have another address for him?"

"No. He's always been very cagey about that." I took my phone out. There were a couple of bars of reception on the screen and I tapped my way to Hoffman's number, trying to marshall my anger so that I could sound reasonable rather than irate. A tinny voice told me that it was out of service.

"Nothing." I shrugged at the others. "He must have been using a burner to call me. But look at it; the house empty, acid conveniently to hand. He bloody planned this."

I turned away, looking out across the overgrown gardens, the once immaculate lawns now neglected and returning to the wildness of the bush they'd been created from, and I took a couple of deep breaths.

For months I'd been negotiating this handover, fitting

our arrangements around all of Hoffman's fears, reassuring him that no-one planned to arrest him. I'd changed flights several times as he prevaricated and although we'd spoken the day before, part of me had been expecting a call that morning, calling the whole thing off or delaying a little longer. Instead, he'd decided to destroy this painting that he claimed was a family treasure with sentimental attachments. The cruelty of it was striking. On an infinitely smaller scale, it seemed the apple hadn't fallen far from the tree.

As I blinked away angry tears I didn't want anyone to see, I felt a hand on my shoulder.

"Come on, Kate. I'm not keen to hang around here. He could come back and there's no point looking for trouble." Pete's tone was sympathetic if pragmatic.

"Yes, okay." I turned back and looked at the wreck of a painting. "Have we got something to flush this with? And a bag? I need to take what's left with me. You never know, it might be a fake but I'll have to get it checked out."

Wearing the latex gloves I'd shoved in my pocket earlier, I soaked the canvas with as much water as we could spare on such a hot day, hoping to dilute the acid to a level where it could be handled, albeit with care, and with what used to be—still was, in the absence of expert assessment, I supposed—a sodden Renoir chucked into a carrier bag one of Pete's mates found in the back of their truck, we returned to our vehicles.

I wasn't saying much and my anger must have been palpable judging by the wary looks the three men were giving me, in between scanning our surroundings for any sign of Hoffman. Sweating inside my Kevlar, I went to rip open the Velcro but Pete shook his head.

"No. We'll go back to where we stopped earlier and stow

everything away there. Just in case he's nearer than we think. He may have hung around to watch what happened."

"If we see him, I'll fucking shoot him." I got into the Land Cruiser and put my head in my hands for a few seconds, wondering how I was going to break the news to the Larssens.

I couldn't even give them what was left; that would add heartbreaking insult to what had already been seventy-odd years of injury. It wasn't news to pass on in a phone call. I would have to go to The Hague and tell them in person that this touchstone of their family had gone for good.

I'd get the remains tested, find out if Julius had indeed destroyed the original. If it was the Renoir, then that was a tragedy. If it wasn't, and Julius Hoffman was trying to con me, then I hoped he had the sense to keep a low profile because I'd be coming for him.

2

Sipping a glass of icy Stellenbosch Chenin Blanc, nibbling salted almonds, and scrolling through emails on my phone, I tried not to dwell on the utter disaster of my day. All this work and I was going home with the remnants of a Renoir, damaged way beyond any restorer's skills. And maybe not even that. The possibility that it might be a forgery and that the original was still safe wasn't enough to cheer me up and it was hard not to blame myself. Endlessly, I ran through the conversations I'd had with Hoffman, wondering whether I'd messed up somewhere.

When we got back to the hotel, I'd said goodbye and thanks to Andy and Wally, reminded them to send me their invoices, and gone up to my stuffy room. After a shower, I'd changed into a sleeveless top and a long wrap skirt, left the painting in a bath of cold water with a note for housekeeping warning them not to touch it, and adjourned to the bar which seemed to be the only part of the building with decent air-con. It was mid-December, Slade were playing in the background wishing everybody a merry Christmas, but I felt anything but festive.

"You okay?" Pete took the barstool next to me, his voice concerned. He knew how much I'd cared about this job and must have realised that taciturn wasn't what I needed in a drinking buddy tonight.

His hair was rumpled, still a little damp from the shower, and the whiteness of his linen shirt was made even brighter by the tan he'd acquired in just a couple of days of South African sun. Pete smiled, hazel eyes on mine, and I felt an unexpected pang as I realised how much I missed waking up to that smile. My heart sank. An evening of Pete being warm and funny wasn't what I needed. I'd almost rather we returned to the brooding silence we'd driven in all day.

"I'm not feeling especially cheerful, to be honest. Getting a bit drunk seems like a good option." I took a mouthful of wine, not smiling back. "I'm contemplating my life choices. Maybe Kolya was right and it's time to hang up my body armour and concentrate on shopping for rich people."

"Ah. Not going well there?"

"We broke up. Didn't you know?"

"Joe said something." Pete shrugged a little. Joe Cathcart, insurance underwriter to the super-rich had introduced us when I needed armed back-up recovering a stolen artwork that had ended up in Belarus. I'd mentioned that Kolya and I had split up when I had lunch with Joe a week or so earlier. Joe's wife, Ellie, was Pete's cousin so I was pretty sure that what Joe knew, Pete knew. Not that the sorry state of my love life was exactly top secret.

"It was after the Sokolov business. Kolya seems sure it's simply a break while I come to my senses but I don't think I can be the person he wants me to be. Maybe I'm allergic to the idea of settling down." Talking about Kolya wasn't doing much to lift my spirits.

"Maybe he just isn't the right person to settle down with." Pete signalled to the barman and asked for a soda water.

"Quite possibly. Last time I spoke to my mother she made a point of reminding me that I'm not getting any younger and that I'll soon be too old to find a man."

"You're only thirty-four." Pete was smiling.

"That's ancient in her eyes. She wasn't keen on Kolya but now she thinks he was my final opportunity to avoid ending up a lonely spinster with a dozen cats. And then she caught me off-guard and now I'm expected to report home for the Christmas holidays so that she can remind me of this in person." I checked myself and smiled, shaking my head. "Sorry to moan. You don't want to hear all this. I don't want to be thinking about it either."

"What would you prefer to be doing at Christmas?"

"I'm not entirely sure." I looked at Pete, noting his smile and the speculative look in his eyes. "I've been jet-lagged for months and my family isn't conducive to feeling chilled out. I'd think I'd like to be somewhere warm, just sleeping and reading and relaxing, with someone who's good company."

"That can be arranged." There was a glint in his eye.

"Can it?" I raised an eyebrow.

"I have no plans at the moment and I like to think you've enjoyed my company in the past. Why don't we just take off? Mauritius? Hawaii? There must be some piece of paradise available at short notice. You only need to throw a couple of bikinis and a good book in a bag and off we go."

"That sounds tempting." It really did. "But you and me, on holiday together?"

"It'll be like old times."

"Quite." I remembered old times with Pete. Many of them were pretty memorable. "Two rooms?"

"Whatever you want." He grinned, white teeth against his tan and I felt impulsiveness take over.

"Why not? Let's do it."

"Good. Have a think about where you'd like to go. I've always fancied diving in the Maldives. I could teach you."

"Sounds perfect." It did, in many ways, albeit accompanied by a side order of potential complications. "So will you join me in drowning my sorrows now?" I took another sip of wine.

"I don't drink any more."

"Really?" Pete had never been a heavy drinker but that surprised me.

"After you and I called it quits, I had a month or two where I was overdoing it, being a bit maudlin and so on. I didn't go to meetings or anything, just decided to stop." He was very matter-of-fact.

"I didn't realise you were unhappy about us calling it a day."

"It wasn't only that. Work was stressful and it's easier to keep the demons at bay if I don't drink."

"I'm sorry if I hurt you." I reached out, laying a hand on his arm for a moment.

"It's okay." He shook his head as though regretting that he'd shown that wound.

"I didn't realise you felt like that. I thought you saw things as pretty casual too." I was still digesting that Pete hadn't taken my decision to end our liaison with quite the equanimity I'd assumed. It struck me that if I'd known it mattered, that I mattered, so much then maybe I would have acted differently.

"Kate, I haven't been casual about you since the day we met." There was a serious note in his voice. "I just haven't been in a position in my life where I could expect more of you. And you were always very clear that you didn't want anything serious." The look in his eyes was sharply focussed, judging my responses carefully.

"I see." It was true that I'd always maintained that I wasn't interested in commitment. That was down to my history; a violent ex had put me off the idea of a full-time relationship. I thought that Pete, with a nasty divorce in his rear-view mirror, had felt the same. "You didn't tell me that. In the year that we were seeing each other you never said that you would have liked it to be more."

"I'm away so much that it didn't seem fair. And then you ended things and I knew there was a spark between you and Kolya. I wanted you to be happy."

"How noble of you." It was hard to keep the bitter note from my voice.

"Probably the only time in my life I have been." Pete smiled, a little rueful. "If I'd said all this back then, would it have changed your decision?"

"Maybe." I closed my eyes, thinking about that. "Yes, you should have told me. After all, I know about your job, I'm used to always being a bit worried. I knew what I'd be taking on."

"Do you worry about me?" Pete sounded curious, side-tracked by that.

"Of course I do. Every time there's a report of fighting or a hostage being taken near to where you might be. That doesn't just go away overnight. And since we split up, I can't ring you at 3 a.m. because I need to hear your voice and know you're okay." Watching Pete, I saw things I'd never told him and he'd never realised clicking into place.

"I see. You should have said. As should I." He spoke quietly.

"It's a pity you've given up the booze. Now feels like the

perfect time to get drunk and try to forget our mistakes." I smiled, but without mirth.

"Perhaps they're mistakes that can be put right?" Pete leaned in a little closer, his voice low, eyes on mine.

"You think?" I wondered how easy it would be to do that. And realised how much I wanted to.

"Worth trying, maybe?" He half-smiled and I felt my pulse quicken as we looked at each other for a few beats. "I've never met anyone who can take my breath away like you do, Kate."

That brought me up short; a knot in my stomach, the tightness that comes with sudden desire. Pushing my glass away, I reached out, placing my hand on the back of Pete's neck to pull him closer. He kissed me and the familiarity of his lips was like coming home.

We broke apart, our face still close together, both breathing a little faster. I felt too exposed to look him in the eye and dropped my gaze, fixing it on the V-shaped patch of skin visible at the open neck of his shirt. Even with the air-conditioning, it was a hot night and I saw a couple of droplets of sweat there. For a moment, all I could think about was licking them off, wondering what it would be like to once again taste Pete's skin on my tongue. Taking a deep breath, making the decision, I got up and took his hand.

"Come on."

3

Three months later

Scrolling idly through my phone in the lounge at JFK, I spotted the email in my inbox beneath one from my sister. The sender's name, *Keeping An Eye On You*, was all too familiar, and the subject line *"You're looking good"* stood out. Sighing, taking another slug of airport coffee, I tapped on the message to open it.

I knew what to expect. A sentence or two of text, sometimes curt but often pretty vicious, usually accompanied by a photo of me from a couple of years earlier. Walking on the beach, drinking wine in the summer sunshine, and so on. These arrived every few weeks and the sender was my ex-boyfriend, Chris. The ex who'd served time for assaulting me. The ex who'd been kept away from me by a restraining order that had expired a few months ago. The ex who refused to back off, presumably because of some twisted desire to make sure that I would never forget what he did.

As if I would forget the rage and the injuries he left me with.

Refusing to let it affect me, I had a routine. I filed the messages in a folder labelled "Scum" just in case I ever needed to produce them, blocked the email address, although that never worked because he used a new disposable one every time, and I moved on, determined not to dwell on it. At first, the emails scared me, bringing back waves of fear, but now I was bored by them, wishing he'd get on with his life and leave me alone.

But this email was different.

The photograph attached was of me, but this time it wasn't one taken during our relationship. Instead, I was outside the big black front door of the Georgian townhouse that contained my flat. Judging by the way I was standing; feet apart, hands on thighs, leaning forward as though to catch my breath, I'd been out for a run and finished by sprinting up the steep hill of Dundas Street. To take this, Chris must have been spying on me.

Feeling a sudden chill despite the overheated air of the airport lounge, I enlarged the image, looking for a clue as to when it had been taken. My running gear wasn't flashy and the black leggings and thin fleece could have been any of a dozen or more days in the last month. Nor did the rain narrow it down—there was no point being a fair-weather runner in Edinburgh. The cobbles showed that Chris had been on the other side of the street and a metallic blur in one corner indicated that he'd been positioned between a couple of my neighbour's cars so I'd be less likely to spot him.

It seemed that ignoring Chris' emails had only provoked him into escalating things, getting closer, taking it up a notch to get a reaction from me. I wasn't going to let him have that satisfaction. Leaving the court after he was convicted and given a prison sentence, I'd put Chris firmly out of my mind and tried not to give him another thought.

Instead, I had thrown myself into my work, pulling off a handful of pretty spectacular recovery jobs—a van Gogh and a Goya among them—and I'd taken on a new consultancy client in the States who had the ambition and the finances to build an art collection second to none. Two years on from Chris's assault, I'd never been in a better place, professionally. And relationship-wise, things were great with Pete now that we were back together, despite spending so much time apart.

Looking at Chris's message again, I bit my lip. If ignoring him wasn't working, I'd have to do something more proactive. Opening a new email, I composed a note for the lawyer who'd organised the now-expired restraining order, suggesting we talk about my options. Could I get that reinstated? Was sending these emails even an offence? And, I wondered with a shiver, what was he going to do next?

TEN HOURS LATER, the cab pulled up at my flat on Great King Street. I took a deep breath as I paid the driver and got out, not letting myself scan the street. If Chris was lurking somewhere I was damned if I'd allow him to see me looking nervous. Nevertheless, I asked the cabbie to wait until I was inside before driving off and heaved a sigh of relief when I let the latch on the outside door fall behind me.

Inside, I took a quick look round. It was months since Yuri Sokolov, frustrated I'd spotted that his stolen Mark Rothko painting was a worthless forgery, had sent his thugs to vandalise my flat as part of some twisted idea of payback. Despite being pretty certain that he'd be keeping his distance now, I seemed to have fallen into the habit of checking each time I came home, not wanting to experience the gut-punch of unexpected destruction again.

But everything was as I'd left it, right down to Arthur, who stalked out of my bedroom and regarded me with a look of utter disdain, every molecule in his feline body resenting my very existence.

Arthur had unexpectedly come with the flat, just like the white goods and the previous owner's stash of porn mags on the top shelf in the box room, and I hadn't the heart to take him to the Cat and Dog Home. We existed in a Cold War state, neither pushing our luck with the other, and maintained a level of mutually resentful civility. Except when Pete was there. Arthur loved Pete in a way that felt like a personal insult, relegating me to a mere household functionary.

I took a long shower to wash off the grime of a day of New York streets and airports, put a load of washing on and sorted my dry cleaning. A week of meetings with clients, art dealers and auction houses on both coasts had been tiring and although I knew I should write up the pages and pages of notes I'd taken and turn them into specific, actionable plans, I decided it could wait. Glad of the break from needing to be groomed and well-dressed, I pottered about the flat in leggings and an old Coldplay t-shirt, a baggy cashmere cardigan with a moth-eaten cuff over the top.

Just as I was rootling through menus, wondering what to order for dinner, there was a knock on the front door. Not the outside street door, so I assumed it must be Flora, my cat-feeding upstairs neighbour who I'd texted to say that I was back. Perhaps she'd fancy an evening of takeaway and gossip?

Padding across the hall to let her in, a greeting already

on my lips, I stopped short. What if it wasn't her? What if it was Chris? What if skulking about waiting to take a photograph of me wasn't enough for him? I remembered the last time he was in my flat, blacking out as he squeezed my throat, and felt the hairs on the back of my neck rise.

I pressed my eye to the spyhole, telling myself that I was being ridiculous, and gasped in surprise before yanking the door open.

It was Pete.

Pete who was supposed to be ensuring the safety of an American news crew in Syria and who I was sure had been there when we'd spoken the night before, given the shaky connection and the chatter of other languages in the background. Still wearing combat trousers and dusty boots with a heavy jacket, he'd obviously left work and not even stopped to change before catching a plane out.

"You!"

"Me." He was grinning broadly, pleased at having caught me out.

"What are you doing here?"

"I swapped some time off with Tommo and couldn't think of anyone I'd rather spend it with. Fourteen hours, one helicopter ride and a plane later, here I am." He shrugged as though it was nothing.

"You're crazy." I shook my head as I stepped forward to kiss him.

"Very probably. Now, are you going to invite me in?"

A COUPLE of hours later I went into the drawing room with our takeaway. Pete was standing by the window, barefoot now in jeans and a t-shirt. He'd lit a fire and was looking out into the darkness at the sandstone townhouses opposite. A flicker of disquiet ran down my spine, wondering if Chris was out there, watching, but I batted it away.

It was a lovely room with a parquet floor and white walls hung with artwork I'd picked up for a song over the years. There were bookcases across the entire back wall, a massive navy linen sofa and a marble fireplace with huge baskets of logs either side.

Although not an especially feminine space, looking at Pete I was struck once again by the incongruity of him in it. He was well-spoken and had perfect manners, was gentle and warm, but he had a raw physicality that always stood out. It was like having a wolf in my drawing room. I liked it very much, but sometimes I worried whether that tension, that spark, might wither away if we had a more conventional, full-time relationship.

"Dinner's up." I laid the pizza boxes on the coffee table with a stack of paper napkins. Pete folded the old wooden shutters across the window before coming to join me. He bent to kiss me and I smiled, glad to have him back for so many reasons. I curled up, feet tucked in beside him and took a slice of ham and mushroom pizza. Arthur appeared and curled up on the other side of him, glaring across at me as though I was the interloper. Pete gave him a piece of ham and Arthur purred.

"Here." Halfway through our takeaway, my phone bleeped and Pete passed it to me. It was my mother. Not in the mood, I sent the call to voicemail.

"You're avoiding calls from your mum?" Pete took the last piece of pizza. "Is that wise?"

"Probably not. But she's been nagging me to go and visit for a while and I'm running out of excuses. Several times since I skipped Christmas, she's pointed out that she's fed up of reminding Anna's kids who I am. Even my fleeting visit at New Year wasn't enough to mollify her."

"I thought she didn't mind about Christmas?"

"At the time she said it was okay. Anna and Olly already had plans to visit his parents in Bath so it would have just been the three of us. Mum and Dad booked tickets for a last-minute cruise. They enjoyed it, but it seems I'm in the wrong all the same."

"Does she know where you were?" Pete grinned, obviously remembering what a wonderful time we'd had in the Maldives.

"Yes, but I was vague about who I was with. She did ask what I could possibly be doing that was more fun than spending time with my family. I was tempted to send her a picture of you lying in bed with just a strategically placed sheet and the message 'he was a lot more fun' but I thought better of it. Mum wouldn't have found it amusing and I'd have had to answer dozens of questions."

"You could simply tell her you're seeing someone and leave it at that." He shrugged, reaching out and stroking my leg.

"However casually I mention our relationship to Mum it will trigger Inquisition-level questioning."

"Would you have to say much? Stick to a few facts, keep it banal. It's not as though she's going to waterboard you." Pete leaned over to pick up the bottle of wine and topped up my glass.

"True. But she'd want to know all about your background, what you do for a living, why you're still single, what went wrong with your marriage, what we're planning for the future, how can we possibly settle down when both of us are travelling all the time. I'm exhausted just thinking about it."

"There's not much to say about me. Don't mention the regiment, just stick to the Paras like I usually do. And you needn't tell her a lot about Karen, only that she left me while I was deployed and a year later while I was away supposedly defending our freedom again, she buggered off to Australia with the kids to marry her new bloke. Your mum's bound to be sympathetic about that."

"She definitely would be but it's still easier to say nothing."

"One day you'll have to tell her." He smiled. It may not have been explicitly acknowledged, at least by previously commitment-phobic me, but we both saw our relationship as long-term.

"I know. Mum just worries. She thinks I'm afraid of men because of what happened with Chris." I sighed, no longer amused as I remembered that last argument and the email that had arrived earlier.

"You've never felt nervous around me, have you?" Pete laid his hand over mine, his face serious. "Given my background."

"No, never." I considered his question. "I didn't think I'd want to get involved with anyone else for a long time but that changed as soon as I met you. Even when we've argued, I've never been afraid of you and you wouldn't be sitting here if I had been. Your history's not relevant. Look what Chris did and he's an accountant. You might be able to kill someone with your little finger but you don't have his anger issues." I smiled, wanting to bring this conversation to an end.

"Probably not my little finger. Breaking your pinkie is sore." Pete thought for a moment as he chewed the last pizza crust. "Index finger though—easy. Now, do you have anything in for pudding?"

4

"Ignore it." Pete cupped my cheek, gently turning me back towards him. My phone continued to vibrate on the bedside table. He kissed me, silently promising all kinds of delights, and as he lowered his mouth to my neck, I forgot the ringing phone. It stopped and Pete raised his head, candlelight reflecting in his eyes, wicked grin on his face. "This is why I don't bring my mobile into the bedroom."

"I know. And you know that I normally don't either. But it's there and it keeps ringing and it's making me tense. Wouldn't you prefer me to be relaxed with all my attention on you?" I smiled and ran a fingernail down his spine, heard the hitch in his breath. The phone buzzed. "See, whoever it is has left a voicemail. Why don't I listen to it and if it's something that can be ignored I'll put it in my office and be right back? Anything short of hospitalisation or a stolen Vermeer will just have to wait."

Pete sighed and reached out to pass the phone over. As I tapped the screen to reach the answering service, he kissed his way across my stomach, refusing to abandon his plan of distracting me. I pushed his shoulder and he laughed and flung over onto his back.

"A couple of minutes, that's all." I smiled as I waited for the connection.

"Hello, Kate? It's Caroline Copley here. Beatrice's mother. I'm afraid I need your help." The woman's voice trembled and I sat up, full of the apprehension that comes with a late night message beginning like that. "I probably shouldn't have called so late. I'm panicking a bit, you see. It's probably nothing and I know this sounds mad, but Beatrice has disappeared. Her office said she was on holiday but they were expecting her back by now. And she didn't tell me that she was going away. I thought that she'd just forgotten..." Caroline's voice tailed off for a moment and then she seemed to pull herself together, her tone brisker.

"You see, I don't know any of Bea's friends apart from you and I wondered whether she'd been in touch with you. I can't get a response to emails or texts or anything." Her voice quavered again. "I'm sorry to bother you, Kate. I'm sure you're very busy but I'm so worried that something dreadful has happened. I don't know what else to do." There was a quiet sob at the other end of the line and my heart went out to her. "Anyway, perhaps you could ring me when you have time. Thanks Kate."

Caroline pulled herself together, finished briskly, and hung up. I stared at the phone for a moment and leaned over to switch on the bedside lamp.

"Vermeer?" Pete asked.

"No. More worrying, possibly." I turned to him. "Listen to this and tell me what you think." I put my phone on loud-speaker and played the message again. When we heard the click as Caroline rang off, I raised a questioning eyebrow at Pete.

"She certainly sounds worried. Is she normally a bit over the top?" He looked serious and I knew I wasn't overreacting to the fear in Caroline's voice.

"It's been a while since we met, but not as far as I recall. Takes things in her stride, I'd have said."

"And Beatrice?"

"Her dad died a few years ago. I wouldn't have thought she would deliberately worry Caroline like this. Perhaps I should ring her in case there's reason she's avoiding her mum's calls?"

"I would. Maybe you can reassure her a bit." Pete got out of bed and pulled on a t-shirt and boxer shorts. "I'll make us some tea."

"Thanks. Sorry. I should have left my phone elsewhere."

"That doesn't matter. This does." Pete dropped a kiss on the top of my head. "Ring her back."

Before I called, I took a moment to think. Beatrice Copley and I had known each other since we started in the upper third at the High School for Girls aged eleven. That was twenty-three years ago. At school, Bea had managed to combine popularity with being highly academic and she was widely expected to go on to great things. She got a first at university, and then went travelling after finishing a master's degree.

In Canada, she met the Kiwi of her dreams and after the obligatory road trip in a vintage VW camper down the west coast of the USA, she'd gone to New Zealand to live with him. We'd kept in touch by email and postcards and the occasional long letter—this was before social media existed and the world was still a big place. She seemed to be having a brilliant time and as far as I could tell, she and Liam were very happy.

When we were younger, Bea was always the more adventurous of the two of us, the confidence that came with that universal popularity, I supposed. I was geekier and my own desire for adventure developed later.

Bea returned from New Zealand rather abruptly, arriving on her parents' doorstep unannounced with her backpack, and it seemed her days of wanderlust were over. She was more sensible, taking a job at a surveying firm that she described as dull, and buying a house on one of the new developments on the edge of town.

Nowadays, I would never have expected her to go off somewhere without telling anyone, certainly not completely off-grid, leaving her widowed mother with no idea where she was going or when she'd be back.

"Hi, Caroline. It's Kate."

"Hello, Kate." The voice on the other end of the line was hesitant. "Thanks for ringing. I didn't wake you, did I?"

"No, it's fine. I wasn't asleep." It was all I could do not to call her Mrs Copley. "You said that Bea seems to have gone away unexpectedly?" It seemed too dramatic to describe her as missing or having disappeared.

"Well, yes. I'm sorry to disturb you but you're Bea's oldest friend. I thought that if anyone knew where she was, it would be you."

"It's fine. Tell me what's happened."

"That's the thing. I'm not sure, really. I'm probably being silly. But you've always been such a sensible girl." Caroline and I had met no more than half a dozen times since Bea and I left the High School but I supposed I would forever be her daughter's school friend rather than an adult in my own right. "Beatrice just seems to have vanished."

"Are you sure?" I was sceptical, thinking that grown women with mortgages and sensible hatchbacks didn't go missing.

"Yes, it's been over a fortnight now. You haven't seen or heard from her?"

"No, not for a while." I'd only spoken to Bea once in the last six months when I'd called to wish her a happy birthday and I had no idea where she might have gone. It seemed odd that she would be incommunicado, but on the other hand, just because she omitted to tell her mum where she was off to, that didn't mean something terrible had happened. If I kept my mother up-to-date on my comings and goings I'd never be off the phone. "Have you talked to the police?"

"Yes. I visited the police station a couple of days ago but they say they can't do anything. Or won't. She's classed as low risk because she doesn't have problems like mental health issues or a violent partner. Apparently, they aren't able to get involved every time someone decides to take a break from their life. I can see why, but this simply doesn't feel right."

Caroline carried on, explaining the details that both alarmed and reassured her, the things that made her fear her daughter was gone for good and the factors that convinced her that Bea would walk in the door at any moment.

"I can see why you'd be worried."

"But whether something dreadful has happened or not, I can't just wait patiently for news. I'm not sure who to ask for help and I phoned your parents in case Beatrice had told you about her plans. You know Bea better than anyone. And your mother said that you were some sort of investigator."

"Kind of. Part of my job is tracing stolen artworks. I haven't any experience of looking for people."

"Oh." Caroline fell silent and I realised she'd been pinning a lot of hopes on me. "Never mind, I'm probably worrying unnecessarily. I'm sorry to have bothered you, Kate." I heard a quiver in her voice.

"I'm sure she's fine, just being inconsiderate. When she gets back she'll be horrified to realise how much worry she's caused." I tried to sound reassuring.

"People keep saying that but something feels wrong to me. Perhaps it's a mother's intuition." Caroline sounded so sad, as though she knew that bad news, sooner or later, was inevitable, and my heart broke for her.

"Was she seeing anyone? Could she have gone away with them?" I had a vague recollection of Bea hinting at a boyfriend last time we'd spoken.

"No. There was someone, in a casual way, but I think it just fizzled out."

"Okay." I took a deep breath. "I'll message Bea and ask her to get in touch. I'll give it some thought and maybe I can come up with some ideas. Perhaps we should talk tomorrow evening and see if we have any news. Then we'll work out a plan." It seems that I was destined to carry on being Bea's sensible friend.

Caroline sounded calmer and promised to call me immediately she heard anything. I said the same, told her to try and get some sleep, and we both hung up. I leant back against the headboard and pulled the duvet up around me. Pete handed me a mug of tea and got into bed.

"So what do you think now you've spoken to her? Is Bea

missing?" He squeezed my hand and linked his fingers with mine.

"I don't know. I really don't. I can see why Caroline's worried. Bea doesn't seem to have told anyone where she was going. She hasn't been at work and hadn't booked any time off although apparently, her colleagues said that might have just been an admin error. But it's been three weeks and surely she'd be back by now?"

"You'd think. Would it help if you went down there?"

"Maybe. It would help Caroline I think, but I'm not sure what I can actually do. And I'm jet-lagged and you're only here for a couple of days. I don't want to chase off down south if Bea's playing silly buggers. Knowing her, she'll walk through the door as soon as I get there." I shook my head, torn between worrying about Bea and being annoyed with her for being so selfish.

"I'm going back on Sunday but I'll understand if you need to go." Pete kissed my shoulder. "This is more important."

"No." I decided. "I'll do as I said. See if I can think of anywhere she might be, message Bea and try to persuade her to get in touch with her mother, and we'll see where we are tomorrow. I'll maybe drive down on Sunday." I spoke firmly, drawing a line under my equivocation. Then something struck me. "If you're coming home next week, why have you come back for a couple of days now? It must have cost you a fortune."

"It did but are you complaining?" Pete smiled, stroking my hair away from my face.

"Not at all. It's been weeks and I've missed you, but a trip home for less than 48 hours seems a lot of trouble to go to simply to surprise me."

"It was a spur of the moment thing. I had some free time

and just felt the need to hold you and tell you how much I love you."

"I love you too. And it's wonderful to have you here." I switched off the lamp, the bedroom once again lit only by candles, and turned to kiss him.

5

Pete could sleep anywhere, at any time. Cat-napping was a skill he'd acquired in the Army. If you never knew when you'd be called on next, when you'd get the chance to rest or what you'd be doing, I supposed you learnt to grab some kip whenever possible. So while I fidgeted and watched the numbers flick round on the clock radio, preoccupied with Caroline's phone call, Pete slept beside me like the proverbial.

At 3 a.m., I gave up and slid out from beneath his arm, pulled on a dressing gown, and went through to my office. Sitting down at my desk, I flicked the mouse and blinked in the darkness at the blueish glow of the screen.

For all that I'd tried to reassure Caroline, the truth was that Beatrice's disappearance worried me. Logically, I knew she'd probably just taken off on holiday, forgotten to tell her mother, and her employers had muddled up the dates. Thoughtless sure, but I couldn't believe that there was any more to it than that. Women in their thirties with nice, normal lives didn't vanish into thin air. Or was it that I simply refused to consider the alternatives?

I opened my email, glad to see that there wasn't another from Chris, and sent a brief message to Beatrice:

"Hi there, I hope you're having a great time on a beach somewhere beautiful or climbing Kilimanjaro, but you went off without telling anyone when to expect you back. I know she's probably overreacting but your mum called me and she sounded worried so can you let her know everything is okay? Talking of when you come home, Mum's nagging me to visit. I'll drop you a line when we fix a date and let's catch up over dinner and too much wine. Love Kate x."

I sent a virtually identical message to her phone and sat back, at a loss for what else to try given Bea's stubborn refusal to use any sort of social media. I half-expected a reply in ten minutes promising to call Caroline and attaching a photo of some beautiful beach. But the part of me that was uneasy wasn't surprised that nothing landed in my inbox.

Unable to do more for now but still not sleepy, I settled down to work through my emails. I didn't find anything particularly exciting lurking there. No more from Chris, thankfully. Various art trade newsletters. A gossipy message from a London dealer letting me know about a Manet he was looking to move on discreetly for a collector with cash-flow problems and which he thought might be of interest to the Impressionist-loving oil magnate who was one of my clients.

There was a rather curt missive from someone at Interpol asking me to ring –them—I knew what that was about and it could wait, being entirely for their benefit rather than mine.

Joe had dropped me a line with an update about a recent theft, hoping there would be a ransom demand soon before the painting disappeared into the underworld completely, maybe never to return.

And there was one from my mother, telling me to expect a call from Caroline. I answered a few, deleted others, and left the rest for later. Yawning, I pushed thoughts of Bea from my mind and went back to bed.

I WOKE about nine to a clunk on the bedside table as Pete put a mug of coffee down and a shift of the mattress as he climbed in next to me. Eyes still closed, I snuggled close. Waking up with him was one of my favourite things.

"Do you have any plans today?" he asked and I felt his lips brush my hair.

"Nope. I even dealt with emails in the middle of the night so I have nothing I need to do." I stretched and opened my eyes. "You have any suggestions?"

"Well, we could just stay here in bed, but the sun's out so how about a walk on the beach?" He smiled. "I feel a bit restless, in need of fresh air."

"Sounds good. Stop for breakfast on the way?"

"Absolutely."

A COUPLE of hours or so later, after a pit-stop in the cafe at Archerfield for eggs Benedict and more coffee, we were walking in the crisp, cold sunshine along Yellowcraig Beach in East Lothian, miles of drum-hard sand beneath our feet, dunes to our right, the islands of the Firth of Forth to our left. It was a favourite place. In fact, we'd come here the first time Pete visited me in Edinburgh.

"Remember when you first brought me here?" Pete took

my hand. "I knew I'd never get bored of walking along beaches with you."

"That's sweet."

"Isn't it? Don't tell my mates." He grinned. "It's been a good couple of years. On the whole."

"Really? Even with a gap?"

"Even with that. Kolya was just a phase you needed to go through. I knew you'd realise we should be together."

"Don't be smug." I turned and lifted my face to kiss him. "I saw Kolya last week. Just for lunch to discuss some pieces he's interested in that are coming to auction."

"Did he beg you to reconsider? Try to seduce you?" The tone of Pete's voice didn't change and I was glad that he wasn't threatened. Kolya had been a client before our relationship and I hoped to avoid any awkwardness now that it was over.

"No. Kolya doesn't beg. He was the perfect gentleman. He asked after you, as if he was testing the water a little. And I told him it was going well, that we were very happy. I'm sure he'll meet someone else soon at one of the endless galas and first nights he goes to."

"Sounds much more glamorous than when we met, eh? Minus ten temperatures and wearing thermals."

"No. But I wouldn't change that. Meeting you was an unexpected bonus of that trip." I smiled, remembering.

Despite the danger of our excursion to recover the stolen van Gogh, it had all come together perfectly and when I held the precious painting in my hands, I'd felt the rush I always did when I recovered a piece. That surge of adrenaline was undoubtedly responsible for what happened later. Driving to the hotel to pick up our gear before heading to the airport, Pete had been beside me in the back of the jeep and my every nerve-ending was tingling.

The plan was to take the owner's jet back to Geneva to return his van Gogh and it seemed the most natural thing in the world for Pete to hitch a ride with me. We spent a weekend there and fell into an involvement that I refused to call a relationship but which kept us both happy for about a year until I wondered whether it was time to look for something more conventional.

"So you'll be back from Syria in a week or so?" I asked.

"I reckon. It's only some meetings and a hand-over. Then I'm taking a few weeks off."

"Any plans?"

"Apart from seeing as much of you as possible? I've been wondering if I should make some changes so I thought I'd look up some old comrades, do some hill-walking. That sort of thing."

"I can't see you running team-building days for middle-managers who think they're tough." Pete and his mates often joked about their relative lack of transferable skills and the routes many of them took.

"Well, no. But I've had enough of deserts and people threatening to shoot me so it's time to give it some thought. Maybe we could spend a week or two at my place in Cornwall? See what ideas we can come up with."

"That would be great. In the meantime, I think I'll go down to Worcester for a few days." Beatrice, and her whereabouts, were still playing on my mind. She hadn't replied to my messages and I was starting to feel uneasy.

"You think Caroline's right about Bea?"

"Maybe. Logically, I know it's unlikely, but it's niggling at me. If the police won't take action and Caroline doesn't know where to start, at least I can try to help. I told Caroline that missing people aren't my area, but my skills might be all we've got at the moment. If I find a reason to be worried, then perhaps I'll be able to persuade the police to do something."

"So, where are you going to start, Sherlock?"

"At her house. Look for bank statements to see if they show which beach in Bali she's sunbathing on. Maybe I can get access to her phone, computer, email, that sort of thing. Ask people at her office if she said anything about places she fancied visiting on holiday. Find out if she was seeing someone, who she's been socialising with lately. What do you think?"

"Sounds as though you've got plenty to go at. And if you can spare the time, you're probably the person who'll be of more practical use. Your background is more relevant than most people's and you're certainly nosy enough." He grinned. "What does your gut tell you?"

"My gut says go."

"Then go. But maybe not until tomorrow?" He dropped a kiss into my hair. I looked up to see him smile and the twinkle in his eye that was hard to resist. "It was a long flight back here and it cost me a fortune and a couple of favours."

"Aren't I worth it?"

"Always, Kate. Always." And we carried on walking, the wind at our backs.

WE SPENT the afternoon at my flat, lazing around before stirring ourselves to go out for dinner. I kept checking my phone for a message from Bea that never came but on the whole it was one of those peaceful, aimless Saturdays that were so pleasurable. I reflected on Pete's comments regarding a change of job. More weekends like this would be good, less of the pressure from airline schedules and warzones. And I wouldn't worry about him as much because at present each time he went back to work I wondered whether this was the trip where his luck would run out.

6

Turning onto the M74, I tried to put aside thoughts of how I wasn't looking forward to being nagged by my mother about all aspects of my life, or the amount of work I really should be focussing on with the spring sales looming, the gaps in my clients' collections and the millions burning holes in their pockets.

Instead, I found myself thinking about Beatrice and what could have happened to her. I'd phoned and texted and emailed again the previous night after I'd spoken to Caroline and hoped that knowing I was driving down to look for her might prompt Bea to tell me she was safe, even if she was ghosting her mother for some reason. But there was no response and I started to get worried.

As I drove, I considered the situation. On the one hand, Bea had every right to take off if she wanted to. But on the other, she wasn't the sort of person to do that. When she was younger perhaps, but since she returned from New Zealand she was more settled. More reliability and less spontaneous travelling, that was Beatrice these days.

We'd started to drift apart when she moved to New

Zealand, but we'd sent emails and postcards and although we didn't know the minutiae of each other's lives, we knew the broad brushstrokes. At least, until she came home, I thought that.

As far as I'd been aware, Liam was the man of her dreams. Living by the sea a couple of hours by ferry from Auckland, they'd run a campsite catering mainly to backpackers. With their early morning surfing, chickens, and organic vegetable garden it sounded like a hippyish paradise. I'd expected that in time they would have kids and Bea would spend the rest of her life in antipodean bliss, her wanderlust satisfied.

Bea's return from this utopia was sudden and unexplained. She and Liam had split up, but she'd just shrugged and said something dismissive when anyone asked why. I didn't know if things had just fizzled out or he'd done something to upset her, she just wouldn't say. If pressed, she seemed to become agitated, so we all dropped it.

I'd expected that after a period to regroup, she'd be off on another overseas adventure. Although neither of us wanted to stay in our hometown, Bea always had a more serendipitous approach than me, convinced that she could head off with a backpack and the universe would look after her.

Instead, with a sensible job and a mortgage, it seemed Worcester was where she'd decided to put down roots again. A nice enough place to do that, but it surprised me all the same. It felt like a dramatic change in personality, but perhaps there came a time when we all had to decide where home was.

For me, life had become less structured and settled. When I was young, I was practical and realistic and all those things you don't want to be at eighteen, but which stood me in good stead getting to where I wanted to be. Now, in my early thirties, with a career and a life I loved, I found myself taking more risks and being more open to adventures. I certainly hadn't worked out where home was yet.

By the time I reached Stafford services on the M6, my shoulders were tense, exacerbated by the weariness creeping through my muscles. I'd set the alarm for six, hoping that I'd leave early enough to avoid the rush hour and regretted it as soon as I woke up. The previous week's travelling had left my body clock in a mess and what I really needed was to be at home, pottering about and sleeping until it righted itself.

Leaving Pete warm and sleepy in my bed was especially hard. So much so, that it had been an hour after my alarm went off that I finally got out of bed. I hoped I'd have this tied up quickly so that I could catch up on work and spend some time with him when he next returned.

Finding my running playlist, I turned the stereo up as I left the services. I might have a lot on my mind but singing along loudly and tunelessly for the last hour or so of my journey would keep me awake and distract me from the stress of going home.

I wasn't sure why I found going back so stressful. Mum and Dad were great, even if Mum did tend to grill me as to why my life isn't running on the lines she'd prefer. And I loved to spend time with my sister, Anna, and her husband and kids. Maybe it was the sense that I'd failed them in some way?

Visiting my family over New Year had been a mistake as my chilled out Maldives Christmas holiday mood faded fast. I'd rung Bea, hoping to catch up and left a voicemail when she didn't answer. She'd replied by text to say that she was sorry but her diary was packed and she didn't have any free time to meet up. I'd been slightly miffed that she couldn't find half an hour for a coffee and hadn't called her in the couple of months since. That moment of pique was probably behind my twinges of guilt and why I was on the road now.

MUM AND DAD lived in a 1920's bungalow about a mile from the city centre. They moved there while I was at university and Anna was at medical school. The first time I visited, I got lost and had to ask for directions. An odd sensation when going 'home'.

There was a bedroom always referred to as 'Kate's room' but it was hard to feel particularly rooted when I had to share it with an exercise bike and a sewing machine. Anna's room became a proper guest room when she settled down with Olly, and I suspected that mine reflected what Mum considered to be my rootless, unsettled life. If I ever got married who knew what it might evolve into.

I parked on the drive and Mum and Dad appeared at the front door, smiling broadly at my relatively unannounced visit. Dad didn't even complain that I'd blocked him in but came out to inspect my car.

"Hello, dear." He hugged me in that rather distant, minimal contact way that men of his age do. "Is that new?"

"Sort of." My Golf was pretty elderly and I kept meaning to trade it in for something smarter, but I rarely used it and somehow never got round to going car-shopping. Instead, Pete had suggested I borrow his rather newer Audi, given that it had already spent several weeks languishing in my parking space at the back of the building.

"Well, it's good to see you driving something smarter. It will give a better impression to your customers," Mum pointed out. I didn't tell her that my only UK-based client was a Ferrari-driving London property developer and I didn't think he'd be impressed by whatever I was driving.

Inside, Mum hugged me again, we settled down for lunch, and for a while it was great to be home. I loved my parents very much and wished I was the daughter they wanted me to be, more like Anna. She was a part-time GP, had two adorable children, lived nearby, and had the perfect husband in Olly, an A&E consultant at the local hospital. I knew my lack of inclination towards either marriage or kids was a disappointment to them, particularly Mum.

"More soup?" Mum held a hand out for my bowl.

"I'm fine thanks. That was lovely."

"I thought we'd have a light lunch and a proper roast dinner this evening. You need to eat properly, especially as you've been travelling. How long were you away for this time?"

"Just over a week. I got home on Friday. They have food in America though. If anything, I've been out for too many fancy dinners."

"You must be exhausted."

"A bit tired. Nothing to worry about. When I travelled from New York to San Francisco and back again I flew private so that was okay. And I took business class flights across the Atlantic so I slept on the plane. Couple of days and I'll be fine." I smiled, hoping to cut off her worries about my health.

"Business class flights and private planes. Such a waste of money. I hope you got some rest yesterday."

"Kind of. But I only fly privately if I'm using a client's plane, not at my own expense. And I like flying in business. It's more comfortable and there's no champagne in economy." I grinned, teasing her, and Dad hid a smile.

"All this gallivanting, Kate. When are you going to get a proper job?" Mum sat down and pushed the plate of cheese scones towards me. "You could open a gallery or something here. There's that lovely one you worked at on Saturdays when you were doing your A levels. I'm sure they'd have you back. Or you could teach art." She smiled patiently, ever reasonable, and I sympathised. She would like nothing more than to have both her daughters living just around the corner.

"Mum, a gallery won't pay me anything like what I currently earn. Besides, I like my job, I like travelling, I like my clients. Well, my consultancy ones, at any rate." Frankly, however choosy I was, I'd be the first to admit that I wouldn't choose to be on social terms with some of the people who hired me to find their stolen artworks.

"I worry about you. Some of those people have you chasing criminals." She pursed her lips and started stacking soup bowls. I sighed; this was a subject we'd covered on several occasions.

"They wouldn't need me otherwise. But let's not get into that again. I shouldn't really talk about it, there are all sorts of legal issues."

"I don't know why you're so secretive." Mum didn't believe in the idea of discretion. If you were circumspect about something, then it was because you're ashamed of it.

"Because my clients want to keep things quiet and sometimes I have to deal with unpleasant people. I like to keep a low profile."

"So it is dangerous?" She put a spoon down with a clatter and I could have kicked myself.

"Not usually. But art thieves don't have a gentlemanly sense of honour any more than other criminals." I saw the worry on her face and tried to allay that. "I avoid the jobs that appear risky from the outset and if it turns out to look dodgy then I take back-up."

"What do you mean, 'back up'?" She sounded horrified and I rolled my eyes. This wasn't getting any better.

"I know people who work in private security. Ex-Army. I can call on them if I need to. They take very good care of me." I kept my tone breezy, hoping to move the conversation on before she asked too many questions about Pete and his colleagues. It was handy to have a team of mercenaries on speed dial but Mum wouldn't worry any less for knowing that. And if there was the faintest hint of a man in my life, even in a solely professional capacity, she'd want to know all about him. "I'm going to see Caroline this afternoon. I'd better unpack." Time to change the subject.

"Of course. Let's go and do that." It worked just as I'd hoped. Something to do and Mum was up and off to my bedroom before I could blink. Dad winked at me. He knew my life wasn't always canapés and champagne in the world's most exclusive auction houses but he didn't fret like Mum, trusting me not to take unnecessary risks, given that I was a grown-up and all that.

"Caroline sounded really worried about Bea." I rifled through my case, sorting clothes into a chest of drawers.

"She is. That's why I told her to call you. I didn't know what else to suggest. Beatrice always used to be a bit flighty, but I thought she'd settled down when she came home from New Zealand." Mum sat on the bed, smoothing the floral duvet cover.

"So did I. Perhaps she just needed a break from everything."

"But it's so inconsiderate. Her poor mother. I suspect there's a man at the bottom of it."

"Bea was definitely seeing someone?" I remembered the

conversation I'd had with her months earlier and the hints she'd dropped but refused to elaborate on, seeming to hug the information to herself like a precious secret.

"Not that Caroline knew of. But then, daughters don't tell their mothers everything, do they?" Mum gave me a pointed look.

"I suppose not." I wasn't rising to that.

"Do you think you'll be able to find her?" Mum's tone was serious.

"I don't know. Hopefully, I'll spot a clue and it will be clear where she's gone. If not, I'll have to start digging around. But I don't look for missing people, Mum, I chase stolen paintings. I'm not sure there are many similarities. I'll do what I can though. I'd hate to think something dreadful has happened and no-one knows."

"You're a good friend." Mum squeezed my hand and I felt a pang of guilt. For this to happen and for me not to have the faintest clue where to start looking, I really didn't think I'd been a good friend at all.

7

Caroline's house, Bea's childhood home, was a mile or so from my parents' bungalow. Detached, 1930's mock Tudor, neat garden, high hedges, gates on the driveway left open, newish VW Polo parked to one side by the garage. It hadn't changed much since I first visited as an eleven-year-old save for new paint on the front door and the double glazing that had replaced the draughty leaded panes.

I rang the bell and Caroline opened it quickly, a flash of hope on her face swiftly evaporating as she saw that it was not her errant daughter home with explanations and hugs. She still smiled though, and came out to hug me on the front step. Her embrace was heartfelt and I could feel the mixture of desperation and relief in it.

"Thanks for coming, Kate." Caroline hugged me and when we parted her eyes were glistening. I couldn't imagine how terrifying it must be to have your only child seemingly vanish into thin air. "Even if you only reassure me that I'm worrying for no reason, that would help. I keep telling myself that she'll turn up any minute with a perfectly good explanation, but—"

"It's okay." I laid a hand on her arm. "Let's have a coffee and you can tell me where we're at."

Inside, the house was also much the same as I remembered—panelling in the hallway, an old oak settle near the coat hooks, a painting of some boats in a harbour, bought on Mr and Mrs Copley's honeymoon in Devon, if I recalled the story correctly. I followed Caroline through to the kitchen, now fitted with off-white Shaker cupboards and black granite rather than the country pine Bea had grown up with, and she busied herself with a cafetière and mugs.

"No news today?" I hitched a hip on a high stool and took out a notebook in case I needed to write anything down. It was a habit from dozens of visits to crime scenes where paintings had been taken and always seemed to give confidence to owners and curators that I would be able to return their precious artwork. I hoped it would reassure Caroline in the same way.

"Nothing." She placed a mug in front of me and slid a small jug of milk across the island unit. "I can't tell you how glad I am that you're here, Kate. The police took details but I could see they thought I was just fussing. And I can see why they'd think that. She doesn't have the sort of problems that would put her at risk. Beatrice is a normal girl, with a good job and a nice house. So why would she go off like this?"

"They might be right. Maybe she was stressed at work or had a row with a boyfriend and felt the urge to take off for a bit. We've all felt like that and needed a bit of peace on a beach with a book." I wanted to give her some hope but she refused to look convinced.

"I know, Kate, but something's wrong, though. I can feel it. But you're here now and you'll have some ideas, I'm sure."

She had a confidence in my abilities that I thought might be rather optimistic.

"Caroline, I'm not a detective. I don't know what Mum told you but I investigate art thefts. I trace stolen and looted artworks. I've never looked for a missing person before." I tried to sound as gentle as possible but I needed her to understand my limitations. "I'll do everything I can, you know that, but I'm not an expert."

"I know. But you're all I've got, Kate. Anything you can do is a help." Caroline laid her hand on mine, at once desperate and reassuring, the weight of her sadness all too apparent.

"Okay." It was time to be efficient and practical, to see if that made her feel better. "When I last spoke to her, Bea hinted that she was seeing someone. Do you know anything about that?"

"Not much. Like you, I got the impression that there was a man in the background, but she never gave any details and I assumed it had come to nothing. As far as I know, there hasn't been anyone serious since she came back from New Zealand."

"Really?" That surprised me. Bea had been home for a few years now and, intelligent and attractive with long auburn hair, I wouldn't have thought she'd have been short of admirers.

"No." Caroline shook her head and smiled a little. "I used to tell her that she should try to find someone, use one of those dating websites or something, but I don't think she ever did."

"Any problems at work? Arguments, promotions she missed out on, disciplinary actions, anything like that?"

"Not as far as I know. She used to say that her work was routine and a bit boring, really."

"Was she looking to move on from that job?"

"No. I used to suggest it. You know how bright she is, she should be working somewhere that challenges her and uses her qualifications. But whenever I said anything, she would just shrug and change the subject."

We worked through more of the details of Beatrice's daily life, and although I made notes there was nothing that gave me any leads to follow. Whatever was going on wasn't something she told her mother about. I understood that, after all, there was plenty I was discreet about, but I wished Bea had been given to sharing confidences. I would need to keep asking until I found the person who knew the secrets she was keeping.

Caroline emailed some recent photographs over and we arranged to meet at Bea's house the following morning to take a look around, hopefully uncovering the detail that would tell us where she'd gone. With another hug, I took my leave.

Getting into my car, I looked back at the house and saw Caroline watching me; the bright smile of earlier had faded and the frayed edges were showing. A wave of responsibility hit me. I had to find Beatrice for so many reasons; because I wondered if I'd let her down as a friend by not being there when she might have needed me, because she could be at risk, and because I dreaded the thought of having to give Caroline the news that she'd lost her only child.

I GOT BACK TO MY PARENTS' house about five and sighed when I saw my sister's car on the drive. I loved Anna and knew that she and Olly were coming to dinner but I'd hoped that I could chill out, possibly even take a nap and a shower before facing the kids. But as soon as I opened the front door and called hello, I was almost bowled over by a couple of balls of energy.

Four-year-old Alice was sharp as a button, while Jack was two and destined for the England rugby team judging by the way he tackled my legs. I hugged them both, hoisted Jack onto my hip, and let Alice lead me through to the sitting room.

Mum and Anna were drinking tea and giggling. At least, Anna was laughing, Mum was looking less happy. Anna and I kissed and I sat down.

"So, any news on Beatrice?" There was a faintly reproachful tone to Mum's voice and I got the impression she was storing up a grievance.

"No. Tomorrow I'm going to check her house and I'll go to her office."

"You'll have to try hard. Caroline has a lot of faith in you," Mum pointed out, not helpfully, and she left the room to make more tea. It was clear that I'd done something wrong.

"Am I in trouble?" I asked Anna, lowering my voice.

"Not really. Not directly, at any rate. But she's not happy about this." Anna picked up Mum's tablet from the coffee table and flicked it into life. She was grinning broadly as she passed it to me. I looked at her, curious.

"The Sidebar of Shame?"

"Look at the article. Scroll down."

I did. The headline read: *"Ballet legend Nikolai Ivanovich seen in New York with a friend"* and I scanned past the paragraph of text to the photos which were of Nikolai—Kolya—and me. The text didn't say much, just who he was and that we'd been spotted in the Tribeca district where he lived.

I scrolled further. There were six photos, all remarkably similar, showing us walking down the street, standing at a cross-walk, looking in different directions, and then crossing the road together. I hadn't noticed anyone taking pictures and I was amazed that this passed for news.

"So, are you and Nikolai seeing each other again?" Mum returned and handed me a mug, lips tight with disapproval.

"No. But he's still a client. I met him for lunch last week."

"You look very friendly."

"Do we? We're only walking down the street together. Not touching or anything."

"Well, that's something." Mum looked a little mollified. "And at least they don't know your name."

"No, you're described as an 'unidentified much younger woman'." Anna was still laughing, taking care to emphasise 'much'. "Mind you, he's quite something. I wouldn't blame you if you decided to start seeing him again."

"Anna, don't joke. He's far too old for Kate." Mum was annoyed again.

"Is he really?" I asked, curious, leaning back on the sofa and sipping my tea. "He's only just turned fifty. It's hardly decrepit. And as you've pointed out in the past, I'm not getting any younger."

"And he is terribly rich and handsome," Anna added, stirring the pot as only a sister can.

"He's not at all suitable. And he lives in New York." Mum's tone was final.

"True. I could move there though. That's what he suggested when we were together."

"You make a good couple," Anna said, and I looked back at the pictures. Walking and smiling as we talked, both wrapped up against the New York winter in woollen coats and scarves, my dark hair in a loose bun and Kolya greying a little at the temples, I thought she was probably right. But that was very definitely in the past.

"We're not dating again. I promise." I switched the tablet off. "Anna, tell me what you've been up to. And what are you feeding these children? I'm sure they've grown since New Year."

THE EVENING WAS LOVELY, all of us around the same table. Jack sat on my knee and Olly arrived back from his shift at the hospital, bringing wine and more laughter, and for a while, I wished again that I could make myself want the life Mum wanted for me. A small art gallery, a conventional husband, Sunday lunches and Christmas dinner. There was nothing wrong with that, nothing at all, but I couldn't do it, my feet itched at the very idea.

By eight o'clock, I was almost asleep at the table. Olly and Anna bundled the children into the car and bore them home while I took myself off for a shower and bed.

Once there, I regretted the coffee I'd had after dinner and, as the caffeine kicked in, I opened my laptop, watching as my inbox filled up with emails, suddenly nervous in case another one from Chris arrived. But there was nothing and I relaxed again. I also checked my phone. It had been on silent for much of the day but when I listened to my voicemails, it didn't seem I'd missed anything essential. No replies to the messages I'd sent Bea.

I messaged Pete to tell him I'd got back to Worcester safely, that there was still no news of Bea, and that I loved him. A notification from Facebook popped up and I thought yet again that Bea must have an online presence somewhere, even a brief mention that might give me a starting point.

Beatrice Copley is an unusual enough name that I didn't expect to find masses of people and I was right. A decade-old death notice for a woman in Manchester, a mother in Seattle who seemed very active on a PTA committee, and a few other random records from the best part of a century ago.

But not my Bea. Unlike seemingly every other person on earth, she wasn't on any social media platform that I could find. When I googled her email address, all that came up was a small piece on the website of the surveying firm she worked for, but that gave no personal details, not so much as a photo. The only email I found was her work one and Caroline didn't know of another, so I couldn't even take a shot at guessing the password on her email account.

After half an hour, I drew the conclusion that I'd never come across anyone with such a tiny digital footprint. The way information is gathered and aggregated on us these days, I was surprised it was possible to be so invisible, but so far as the digital world was concerned, it seemed Beatrice was a ghost.

8

Jet lag and an unfamiliar bed woke me early and, despite the grey skies and the drizzle, I was out and running by six-thirty. Into the city centre, starting to fill up with delivery vans, round past some my old haunts and then back. The last mile, up a gentle but long slope and into the wind, was a slog. I kicked my trainers off in the porch and went through to the kitchen in search of a cup of tea.

Mum, already up and dressed, took one look at me and flicked the switch on the kettle. The washing machine was running and she'd set up the ironing board.

"Nice jog?"

"Not really. It seemed harder work than usual." I started stretching. "But it's done now, and that's good."

"You had a call about half an hour ago." Mum passed my phone across from the dresser and placed a mug in front of me. "A man called Pete. He was very chatty."

"Was he now? And what did you chat about?" I was wary. My mother can get information out of anyone. All

Pete's training in resisting interrogation would be futile faced with Mum wanting answers.

"I asked how he knew you and he said you worked together sometimes. That he's the 'back-up' you mentioned. So I asked what his background is, to qualify him to do that, and what he did the rest of the time when he's not looking after you."

"And what did he say?" I sipped my tea, guarded.

"He said he couldn't tell me much but that he used to be in the Army. And I asked about his family and he said that he was divorced. So I mentioned that you were single too, just in case he didn't know, and that perhaps he should get to know you better. You know, in a social setting." Mum seemed very pleased by this bit of match-making.

"And what was Pete's opinion of that suggestion?"

"He said that it was a very good idea."

"Interesting. Did he say why he was calling?"

"Not really. He was just ringing to see if you needed any help, I think. And he said to tell you that he should be back in the UK soon and that as he may be in Edinburgh, he'd very much like to have dinner with you. I said you'd call him back to confirm."

"Thanks for that." I bit my lip to hide a smile at the notion of my mother suggesting to Pete that he take me out on a date. If she had any idea what we got up to, she'd have hung up on him. I looked at my messages. There it was:

"Hope today goes well. Good luck at Bea's. Your mum seems nice. I get the impression she thinks I'm the ideal man for you. Dinner next week, I gather? P x."

I replied:

"Thanks. And if you talk to my mother about us again, you won't be sharing dinner or anything else with me. x."

I disappeared before Mum could raise the subject of

Pete again. Half an hour later, showered and dressed in jeans, boots and a leather jacket, I popped my head around the kitchen door.

"I'm off to Bea's house, see if I can find a clue as to where she is. Then I'm going to stop off at Bea's office. And I might be out this evening. I'm not sure when I'll be back."

"Did you call Pete? Really, Kate, you should consider him. He sounded very keen on you. A mother can tell these things. And he's so much more suitable than Kolya."

"You think? Pete's also older than me, also divorced, and he has two kids he rarely sees because his ex-wife moved to Australia. Still think he's ideal?" I smiled, trying to hide my frustration at her desire to have me fit into the pigeonhole she'd chosen for me.

"I just want you to be happy." Mum looked hurt and I felt, predictably, guilty.

"Mum, I am happy. I have a great job and brilliant friends, I get to travel a lot and I have a beautiful flat in a city I love. Even my cat is getting a bit friendlier." I leaned over and kissed her cheek. "Trust me, I'm very content with my life."

"Anna, are you free tonight?"

"I could be. Olly's home. Why?" Anna was brisk; I'd caught her between patients.

"I've suggested to a couple of Facebook friends that we meet up this evening. They're the people I think are most likely to have information about Bea. She doesn't do social media so I don't have a handy list of her own contacts to work through. It would be good to have you there so it seems less like I'm interviewing them. I don't want to let on that Bea's missing."

"Sure. No news?"

"Nothing. I'm on my way to Bea's house so fingers crossed I find a clue. I left Mum and Dad's a bit early though because Mum was, you know, being Mum, so I'm currently killing time and drinking coffee in a McDonald's drive-through."

"All glamour, then."

'Quite. Fewer private jets and less champagne this week. I'll pick you up at eight."

"Fine. By the way," she cut in quickly, "Mum tells me that she's spoken to your friend Pete. Apparently, he sounds very keen on you."

"I should hope he is, Anna. After all, he was still in my bed when I left yesterday morning." And I hung up. We'd have something to talk about tonight for sure, but I kicked myself for letting my own amusement win out over discretion.

I followed up the messages I'd sent to a couple of old school friends and luckily they seemed delighted to have the opportunity to catch up this evening. We hadn't been close friends at school; I wasn't cool enough, but I was tolerated because Beatrice—who was considered cool —liked me.

Their enthusiasm for meeting up was surprising. Maybe they'd also seen the Sidebar of Shame and wanted to see how I had gone from the nerdy girl who sneaked off to art galleries and bookshops to someone who got papped. Or, more accurately, who got to walk down the street with someone who got papped.

Messages from Anna arrived at roughly ten minute intervals, between patients. She was avid to know more about Pete and I knew that in order to buy her silence in terms of not breathing a word to Mum, I'd have to tell her almost everything.

As I neared the end of my coffee I automatically flicked through my emails, making sure no fires had sprung up that needed to be put out. Nothing major, although seeing the messages backing up I was aware that I couldn't just take off for too long. I needed to spend some time looking after my clients soon or they would, quite reasonably, be unhappy.

But there was nothing unwelcome in my inbox and that was a relief. I closed my eyes for a moment, wishing that Chris wasn't yet another problem I would have to deal with.

9

Driving across town that morning was a snapshot of my early life. So many landmarks I remembered from my friendship with Bea: our old school, the café we hung out in, the pubs we got kicked out of at seventeen, the ones that were more welcoming when we reached eighteen, the High Street where we'd made our weekly pilgrimages to buy clothes and makeup. Leaving to go to university after A levels, I'd never returned on a full-time basis and tended, somewhat irrationally, to expect everything to stay the same. Changes, whether in geography or people, always surprised me a little.

Perhaps I should have kept in closer touch with friends from school. Was Mum right when she told me that it was up to me to make the effort because I was the one who'd left? I couldn't shake the feeling that I should have tried harder with Bea and not let our friendship slide. If I had, maybe she'd have been able to talk to me about why she wanted to walk away from her life like this.

The house Bea had bought when she took her current job was a new-build in one of the developments that had sprung up along the bypass. The bypass dated from after I left and the geography of it always confused me; endless roundabouts where I lost my bearings. Today was no exception. I missed the turning twice, cursed, and then found the right one, threading my way between parked cars down the meandering road with its cul-de-sacs on either side, to the end where number 71 sat among its near-identical neighbours.

Five years or so on from construction, the houses showed some signs of individuality—a tree here, a fence along a boundary there, a rash of conservatories.

Bea's car was parked in the driveway. As I walked up the path, just for a moment, I wondered if maybe she'd come home and this morning would consist of laughter and apologies over a cup of coffee. But then Caroline opened the front door, her face pinched and grey, and I knew immediately that there was no good news.

"Hi, Kate."

"Hi. Right, let's take a look round and see what we find." There was no point in small talk, no discussion that would soften the edges of the situation.

Going into the house, I glanced around. Everything looked pretty much as I remembered from the last time I was there, a year or so earlier. Sitting room at the front, dining room at the rear with patio doors to the garden, big archway through to the kitchen, downstairs loo off the hall.

It was stylish in a fairly generic way with comfortable sofas, bookshelves, and a couple of decent amateur paintings in the sitting room. The dining table had a candle in the middle and a few weeks' worth of mail stacked neatly beside it. The kitchen was tidy with a single mug in the draining rack by the sink.

Nothing obvious leapt out at me, but as I looked around

it struck me that although I'd said I didn't look for missing people, only art, the principles were the same. In a gallery or a home, I wasn't looking for the painting that had been lifted. Rather, I was searching for the traces left behind, the details that would lead me to those responsible. Somewhere in this house were clues to where Beatrice was; I just had to find them.

I'd been afraid that I might see signs of violence or a struggle, but it would have at least given me a starting point and a means of getting the police to take Bea's disappearance seriously. Nevertheless, aware that if things turned out badly this could be a crime scene, I took latex gloves from my bag and snapped them on. Caroline looked questioningly at me.

"Force of habit," I explained with what I hoped was a reassuring smile.

The first thing was to see if we could find any indication of how long Bea had intended to be away, if indeed her departure had been planned. The kitchen bin was empty and the contents collected weeks earlier by the dustbin lorry. Perishables had been removed from the fridge, leaving just a few jars of pickles and olives lined up in the door racks. She obviously hadn't left without warning. That was something.

I sorted through the pile of mail—supermarket discount vouchers, a postcard reminding her to make a dental appointment, gas bill. No helpful bank statements or credit card bills but if she was anything like me, that sort of thing was all online. Annoying though, being able to see whether and where she'd used her cards would have saved me time.

Talking of online, I looked around for a computer. Caroline said that Bea had a laptop and that it usually lived in the sitting room but there was no sign of it. I rummaged through cupboards and drawers in case she'd hidden it out of sight when she left, but no joy.

"Caroline, did Bea have a sat-nav in her car?" I asked, a glimpse of her car out of the window reminding me how useful those could be in tracking people's previous destinations.

"No. She didn't like them. Beatrice always used an app on her phone or a paper map."

Checking under sofa cushions, hoping for a handy note or address, I struck gold when I found a small leather appointment diary. I flicked through the pages, heart beating a little faster, only to find that it was full of insignificant details such as when her car was being serviced, her hair cut, or the plumber was booked to call.

Other entries were so abbreviated that they might as well have been in code. "7 – Co Ho" was one of them. She'd scribbled a few phone numbers in the back—mine included—but again, there wasn't much in the way of obvious clues.

As I searched the downstairs rooms, I was surprised by how little clutter Bea had. There was nothing extraneous anywhere. Her house felt as pleasant and impersonal as an upmarket holiday let.

It struck me as odd. My flat was tidy, and one of the offices I had there was utterly immaculate. It was the one for public consumption if I had meetings or talked to clients on Skype, all white walls and good art. But the place where all my files and notes lived was a box room with an overflowing in-tray, a battered filing cabinet, and a pinboard of mugshots and images of missing artwork. Pete joked that it resembled a serial killer's lair.

It was a complete contrast to the rest of my flat but surely everyone, however tidy they were, had somewhere like that where unfiled letters and old receipts festered? Even just a junk drawer in the kitchen? It didn't seem that Bea did, just a few neat folders of paperwork that told me little, apart from the fact that her house insurance was up to date.

I needed to know what she'd taken with her and Caroline hovering at my elbow was making me nervous so I sent her off to check what was missing in terms of summer or winter clothes, whether she'd used a suitcase or a backpack, even what sort of shoes she would be wearing.

One of the card folders was marked "travel" and tucked between some out of date insurance documents, I found her passport. No visa stamps that might indicate recent trips but at least we could be fairly certain that Bea hadn't left the country. It was possible that, like me, she had two passports although that was because I often travelled between countries that weren't keen on each other. Unless that surveying job had got a lot more interesting lately, I doubted Bea needed to.

Satisfied that there was nothing more downstairs to help me, I went up to where Caroline was looking through Beatrice's wardrobes. The smallest bedroom seemed to be where Bea kept the overflow of her clothes and the ironing board, and after a quick and fruitless look round, I started to search the guest room. This was similarly uninformative—empty drawers, a box of Christmas decorations in the back of the wardrobe and a neatly made bed. No clues.

In the landing, after fruitlessly checking the airing cupboard, I noticed the hatch into the attic. Maybe she kept papers that would reveal her current location up there. There was a pole to pull down the hatch but no ladder. I took a chair from the spare room and climbed up. Balancing on the edge, I pulled out my phone and switched on the torch. It was completely empty, not so much as a mousetrap.

I dropped back down and turned to her bedroom,

hoping that this most private of spaces would yield something. Searching there felt awkward, especially with Caroline next to me—there are things your oldest friend might merely raise an eyebrow at but which your mother never needs to know about. I hovered in the doorway as Caroline rifled through the hangers in the wardrobe.

"It's winter clothes she's packed. Jerseys, thermals, that sort of thing. And her walking boots aren't in the cupboard downstairs. Bea has a purple waterproof jacket and it's not there. I don't think she's using a suitcase either. She has a kind of holdall on wheels and that's not here." Caroline closed the doors and looked at me hopefully.

"She's prepared for bad weather then, that shows some planning. If she hadn't taken anything I'd be more concerned." I smiled. "I'll go through this room, shall I?"

"That's fine. I'll leave you to it. The houseplants need watering and I was going to call on the neighbours again." Caroline left and I set to work.

Our bedrooms were where we let down our defences, physical and emotional. By my reckoning, if Beatrice had secrets, this was where I would find them. And she definitely had secrets, I was sure of that. No-one's house was this impersonal unless they were concealing something. I was pretty certain she wasn't an embedded CIA operative, so what was she hiding behind this carefully anonymous exterior?

Finding a vibrator, lube, condoms and a handful of erotic novels in Bea's bedside drawer made me glad I hadn't started searching with Caroline looking over my shoulder. Also in there was an oldish iPhone. I turned it on and it fired up and then shut down immediately. It was out of battery life but must have been used relatively recently. I put it on the bed to take away and look at later.

Starting on the chest of drawers near the en-suite bathroom, I found makeup and jewellery in neat plastic containers, sorted and organised, in the top drawer. Second and third drawers contained underwear. Bea was evidently keen on matching sets, all coordinated and folded tidily. All uniformly tasteful and decorous, unlike my own which ran the gamut from practical M&S multipacks to expensive silk indulgences and was rarely arranged neatly. Below that was a drawer of precisely folded t-shirts and another of gym gear.

But I was still looking for the clutter, the personality, the things she kept out of sight. I lifted the valance on the bed and slid open the drawers underneath, hoping that this might be her junk drawer, the equivalent of my box-room office, hoping for a hint as to the intimate details of Bea's life that she seemed to be hiding so well. It might not have been a clue, but it was definitely intimate and quite a surprise.

Immaculately folded and organised, like everything else, was an array of lingerie diametrically opposed to the matched sets in her drawer. Latex, leather, corsets—stuff I would never have imagined her choosing and which really didn't fit with the lack of personality displayed elsewhere in her house or her wardrobe. She obviously had a partner that Caroline didn't know about. Definitely a man, judging by the condoms, and clearly one whose tastes ran to the tarty.

Closing the drawer, I checked the other bedside table on the far side of the bed. Whoever this man was, he'd been serious enough to be allocated a drawer of his own and it contained two pairs of black Calvin Klein boxers and two pairs of black socks. No fishnet thongs for him, it seemed.

In the en-suite bathroom, I rummaged through the bottles and jars around the sink and the cleaning products and spare loo rolls in the cupboard beneath before finding the nearest thing to a clue in the medicine cabinet. There was nothing very interesting beyond the usual painkillers, birth control pills, and cold remedies. However, not only did the man have a drawer in the bedroom, he'd also been allocated a shelf here containing a razor and shaving gel, a comb and some hair product, and a small bottle of Floris aftershave. I sniffed the contents—citrusy and sharp. Distinctive. I took the comb to the window and squinted. Holding it against my dark sleeve, I saw a couple of fair hairs trapped between the teeth. At last, I knew something about the mystery man in Bea's life. I put it back and shut the cabinet door.

Putting the phone in my pocket, I went back downstairs. What I'd found only seemed to raise questions and the absence of other things raised even more. But something in the phone or the diary might tell me where Beatrice had been, and that might lead me to her.

I DROVE AWAY, considering what I now knew and what I could safely assume. Bea was still in the UK unless she'd managed to acquire fake documents which struck me as improbable. She'd gone away in February, it was now March and she'd taken the time to pack warm clothes. Not just layers, but hiking gear. She planned to be out in the countryside, not walking inner-city streets. The fridge and bin were also empty, which showed either planning or that someone else had cleaned up. I pushed away that second option, not yet willing to think about more sinister possibilities.

Before leaving I'd searched her car but there were no clues in the door pockets or glove box or slipped under the seats. I'd even checked beneath the spare wheel's cover in case she'd hidden anything there. All I came up with was a half-empty tube of hand cream and a Kit Kat wrapper. I thought of my car and the detritus that littered it and wondered again how Bea managed to keep anything personal so well hidden.

It struck me that maybe she'd hidden everything because she expected people to come looking for her and she didn't want to give them any clues. But why would she do that? What on earth could she be involved in that would make her so careful?

On the other hand, if this wasn't Bea's doing and she had come to harm, someone had done a good job of tidying up afterwards and why would they take her clothes and so on? I thought it was pretty safe to assume Bea had left of her own volition. But her car was on the drive so she was either using public transport, had hired another vehicle, or was with someone who had a car. And who might that be?

I suspected that the man she'd hinted at last time we'd talked was still around. Or perhaps he'd been replaced. Whoever he was, he had overnight stuff there so it must be an involvement of some standing, not a brief fling. And he was probably the man who liked to see her in that underwear because I couldn't imagine Bea keeping it if the relationship was over. It didn't strike me as stuff she'd choose to wear. Everyone made exceptions sometimes but that drawerful was a lot of exceptions. No, I reckoned that relationship was a few months old and still going strong.

I'd spent a couple of hours in Bea's house and I had little to go on. She was a woman who didn't give much away, even in her own home. The phone and the diary were my starting points. Hopefully one of them would be the loose thread that I could pick at until the whole thing unravelled.

10

The company Bea worked for—MacGregor and Wise—had offices a few miles and half a dozen roundabouts from her house, in one of the business parks that seemed to be proliferating along the bypass. A glance at their website while I drank more takeaway coffee in a supermarket car park revealed that they were surveyors who specialised in brownfield and semi-industrial sites, looking at possibilities for housing and so on.

For all that it might be fascinating for some people, I wouldn't have expected Beatrice, who travelled the world in search of adventure, who necked flaming tequila shots, who crossed the globe for love, to have stayed here so long. It must be seven or eight years, I realised. That woman, bold and courageous, had settled for redeveloping factories into housing estates. It didn't seem to fit.

The reception was spacious with a couple of leather sofas and framed photographs of MacGregor and Wise's projects. At least, I guessed that's what they were; one corrugated steel warehouse or starter home estate looked much like another to me.

An immaculately made-up receptionist—Stacy Hamilton, according to her name badge—smiled at me from behind her wood and glass desk. The professional smile was tinged with curiosity. I doubted that I looked like someone with an old factory to redevelop.

"Hi," I began in my most charming manner. "I wonder if you can help. I'm a friend of Beatrice Copley's and her mother is a little concerned about her as she hasn't heard from her for a couple of weeks. I'm sure it's just a mix-up of holiday dates and Caroline's worrying about nothing. Can you check for me, please?"

I expected Stacy to be helpful. After all, this was a relatively small office with no more than thirty vehicles in the car park and I guessed that everyone would know each other. I hated working in an office and only did it for a couple of years or so, but I remembered how people used to gather around the coffee machine or a table in the nearest pub to discuss holidays and boyfriends and nightmare clients. Stacy may not know Beatrice well, but she was a colleague and even if she couldn't help me, surely she'd be a little concerned? However, Stacy looked surprised by my question, wary even.

"Oh. Another friend of Beatrice's was here last week. It seems everyone is looking for her." Stacy didn't sound like she was a fan of Bea's. "Can I take your name please?" She put her hand on the phone as if to summon assistance.

"I'm Kate Carpenter. Bea and I went to school together." I smiled again, hoping that the person she called would be more helpful.

"But you can't be. Kate Carpenter was here on Friday. I spoke to her. You're not her." Stacy looked even warier now, eyes flicking about as though she felt threatened.

"No, really. I'm Kate. Look—" I fished in the pocket of

my jacket and handed her a business card. "See, Kate Carpenter, art consultant."

"How odd. Let me call a colleague to talk to you." Stacy picked up the phone and asked the person on the other end to come to reception as someone who claimed to be called Kate Carpenter was asking questions about Beatrice. When she hung up, we looked at each other rather awkwardly.

I was curious and completely baffled as to who would do something like that. And worried; it was an odd thing to do. Before I could ask more questions, a door behind her opened and a man appeared. Tallish, slim, with the pale softness of someone who spent too much time indoors at a desk, he was a few years older than me.

"Hello, I'm Gordon Wise." He held out a hand, hesitantly, and I shook it, irritated by its dead haddock quality.

"How do you do, I'm Kate Carpenter."

"So you say." He smiled, but guardedly.

"No, really, I am." I rootled around in my bag and began laying out identification: driving licence, bank cards, even my National Library of Scotland card. "See, photos and everything. I'm Kate."

"I see." Gordon squinted at the random plastic cards, flicked through the creased, much-stamped pages of my passport and looked worried. "Then who was that claiming to be you last week?"

"I have no idea. But I think we need to have a chat."

In my business, checking people's credentials was second nature. I carried a passport or driving licence at all times. My clients were worth billions, so I had to be careful about their personal information too. As for my recovery work, some of the most audacious art thefts in history had been executed in broad daylight by people no-one thought to question.

"So, what did this fake me want to know?" I perched on the arm of one of the leather sofas facing the one where a worried Stacy fidgeted with a bracelet.

"The same things as you. She said that she was trying to find Bea. Apparently Bea's neighbours haven't seen her in weeks so she came here to ask if we knew where she was or what her plans were." Stacy was nearly in tears, fretting at the cuff of her blouse. "I'm so confused. Why would someone use a fake identity? What did she really want?"

Nothing good, I thought, trying to smile patiently while my brain raced. Bea was so private that I couldn't imagine many of her casual acquaintances even knew I existed, so how did they come up with my name? Something else struck me; if Bea had been here then the game would have been up straightaway.

"Tell me, and this is important Stacy, did she ask to see Bea before she gave her name? By the time this woman said she was Kate Carpenter, had you already told her that Bea wasn't here?"

"I'm not sure." Stacy's lip trembled and I try to look encouraging and sympathetic rather than irritated. "I think so." She closed her eyes, and then said, more confidently, "Definitely. She asked if Beatrice was here, and I said no, she was on annual leave. And then, like you, she asked if I knew where she'd gone and when I asked her name she seemed to think for a couple of seconds and then she said it was Kate Carpenter."

A blonde woman in her forties bustled out into reception and sat down beside Stacy, patting her shoulder.

"Perhaps she was a friend of Beatrice's and just had a perfectly innocent reason why she didn't want to give her real name?" The woman glared at me as though I was there simply to upset Stacy and cause trouble.

"Really?" I was sharp. "Why would someone with a valid excuse to be looking for Bea give a false name? Tell me what you think that reason could be." The blonde woman bridled and I got to my feet, out of sympathy now. Gordon Wise was still hovering. He looked less than useful but he was all I had.

"Do you have a security officer? CCTV in reception or in the car park? Anything?" I glanced around. "Do those work?" I pointed to the black cameras on the ceiling.

"Yes, but we don't switch them on." Gordon looked nervous. "And there are no cameras outside. We have a burglar alarm but I don't suppose that's much use is it?"

"No, Gordon. That's no use whatsoever." I sighed. "Did this woman speak to anyone apart from Stacy?"

"Gillian. She has the desk next to Bea's."

"Go and get her." He fairly ran from reception and I waited, impatiently. At work I had a number of personas I adopted to get the information I needed out of people. Sometimes I was friendly and chatty and the gallery girls who'd messed up saw me as someone they could confess their stupidity to. Middle-aged security guards who hadn't been paying attention or who were too slow to stop a thief responded well to a certain amount of sympathy about how hard their job was and would admit their errors. Stressed art dealers bracing themselves for the truly enormous invoice I'd be sending when I recovered their painting felt reassured by breezy efficiency.

But sometimes, when I didn't have the patience to be caring and fluffy to people who've been idiots, it was far more productive to just be intimidating.

I tried that on Gillian and Stacy. I sat opposite them,

took out my notebook and made sure that I looked as official as possible. And it worked.

Between them, they agreed that the woman was well-spoken with a very slight Birmingham accent and was driving a black SUV. She had been wearing jeans and Dubarry boots. Her hair was naturally blonde, she was about five foot two, early thirties, and slim in a curvy sort of way.

"And what did you tell her?" I braced myself, wondering what they knew and how much they'd blabbed.

Not a lot, it turned out. As I'd thought when I searched Bea's house, she was very private and neither of the women, the closest she had to friends at work, had much idea about her personal life. They knew she attended yoga classes at the weekend, knew that she preferred Sainsbury's to Tesco and where she shopped for work clothes. They remembered her father dying a few years earlier but she hadn't talked about it much. Karen vaguely recalled Bea mentioning my name, but no more than that.

By the time I departed, I'd asked around the office to see if any of Bea's other colleagues had information and left my contact details. And everyone was feeling pretty chastened and fully briefed about checking the identification of people who presented themselves asking questions. Gordon had also worked out how to turn the CCTV cameras on. Better late than never, and all that.

"If anyone thinks of anything else, let me know. Anything at all. And if that woman comes back, ring me immediately and keep her here."

"How?" Gordon looked terrified.

"However you like. Tie her up, call the cops, whatever. But do it." I shouldered my bag. "I'll be in touch. Talk to no-one about Bea and make sure you tell everyone else not to."

And I left, gunning my engine down the bypass while I screamed at the steering wheel. I was angry that they'd been stupid and I'd been too late, but I was also starting to feel seriously worried. Still fuming when I got to Mum and Dad's, I sat in the car for a few minutes taking deep breaths while I checked my messages.

It had been a day where I'd hoped to find answers but only ended up with more questions and an increased sense of unease. How could I know so little about a person I considered one of my best friends? Where on earth was she? More to the point, why was someone else looking for her? And who were they?

BACK HOME, I retired to the dining room with a cup of tea and started to flick through the diary, hoping that its cryptic entries would suddenly reveal themselves as clues I could follow, but none of the scribbles leapt out at me.

"Come on, Bea," I found myself muttering. "Where are you? What are you playing at?"

Answer came there none and so I opened my notebook, looking at what I'd jotted down, trying to spot the scrap of information that would give me something to pick at. Again nothing.

But what was most unsettling was the woman impersonating me. I couldn't think of a reason why someone would hide their identity. And why use my name in particular. Was that significant?

The uneasiness I felt was growing. I'd hoped that today would provide answers but instead it had raised more questions. My earlier feelings that Bea was just being thoughtless were fading, now I was starting to be fearful for her.

11

While Mum cooked dinner, I pulled myself together and made a plan. Keep on, keeping on, that was all I could do. The woman who impersonated me may not be important and getting into the phone was the priority. There must be a reason why she kept it tucked away and why she didn't use it in the same way as her usual mobile and my best guess was that it was something to do with whoever the man in her life was. But I wasn't sure how to get into it and nothing I looked at online seemed even vaguely legit.

Still, I knew someone who might be able to help and after waiting for what felt like ages while thousands of masts and exchanges connected us, finally, on a fuzzy line, Pete answered.

"Hey, good to hear from you. How was today? Successful?"

"I'm not sure. I went to Bea's house and her office."

"Any luck?"

"Not really. It feels a bit strange, to be honest." I sketched out what I'd found, or rather not found, at Bea's that afternoon and he listened, interjecting only to clarify a couple of points.

"Any other sign of a male presence, beyond the socks and shaving kit?"

"Not really." I thought about that. "Well, kind of. There was a drawerful of underwear."

"His underwear?"

"No. Women's. I think. God, what if it was his? That's even worse."

"What's surprising? All women have underwear. You've got masses of the stuff."

"Not like this. It was—um—more specialist. Cheap and tacky. I can't imagine Bea wearing lingerie like that. She's the sort who'd buy classier lingerie than that stuff."

"Like you, you mean?" I could hear the smile in his voice. "I never had you down as a prude. Perhaps that's what she likes on the quiet. Or this man of hers does."

"You know better than anyone that I'm no prude. It's probably nothing, but it seemed incongruous and as I have so little else to go on, I'm almost certainly attaching more significance to it than it warrants. If I'd found something useful like a laptop, I'd have just raised my eyebrows at it."

"She had a burner phone in her bedside drawer? And an appointment diary that seems to be in code? Maybe she's on the game?" He didn't sound apologetic for casting aspersions on Bea's character, just practical.

"Pete, this is my oldest friend. She wouldn't do that." But even as I said it, I started to wonder. I had no better explanations.

"How do you know? It always amazes me the secrets people keep. She's obviously hiding something. What's her money situation like?"

"I don't know. There didn't seem to be any bank statements and I couldn't find a laptop or tablet."

"No wads of cash anywhere?"

"Nope. Unless it was very well hidden. I wasn't about to take the side of the bath off or lift the carpets with Caroline there. There was something weird at Bea's office though." I told him about the imposter. He was quiet for a few seconds.

"That's not good."

"No. I mean, I don't think she's a spy out to assassinate me or anything, but why would anyone else be making the same enquiries and not want to let on who they are unless they've got something to hide? And why use my name? Bea seems to have been so cagey about personal information. It must be someone who knows me or knows of me. It feels like too much of a coincidence." I thought for a moment. "The most important thing is that I need to get into Bea's phone."

"There's all sort of software out there but you don't want to risk downloading it. All of it's illegal, most will be full of viruses, and if it doesn't work you could lose everything on there. I know some guys in London but you'll have to take the actual device to them. You could courier it or drive down?"

"No-one nearer? It's at least a couple of hours each way and I'm knackered." The thought of a long trek the next day was not attractive but I'd go if I had to.

"I'll call them; see what they suggest. But don't download anything."

"I won't. I'm not stupid." I felt a flash of irritation.

"No, but you're worried and you might be tempted by a shortcut. Leave it with me."

"Thanks. I love you."

"I love you too." And the line cut out, Syrian communications not being the most reliable.

"Can you walk in those?" Mum appeared at my bedroom door as I was getting ready; Saint Laurent tuxedo jacket, skinny black trousers, diamond ear studs that had been a gift from a grateful client, and the ring that had been my Christmas bonus to myself—the previous year had been a profitable one.

"They're not the comfiest." I looked down at my Louboutin ankle boots. I'd packed in a hurry and they weren't the most practical choice. "I'll be okay if I don't have to run."

"Hmm. You look nice though. Are you and Anna going anywhere exciting?"

"Only to the pub to meet a couple of women that Bea and I went to school with. I didn't tell them I was looking for her, only that I was in town and it would be good to see them."

"I'm sure it will be."

"You reckon? You're more of an optimist than me." I stopped putting on mascara and raised an eyebrow at Mum. "We're just Facebook friends, people that used to know each other a long time ago. They might be useful, that's all."

"Do you think something bad has happened to Bea?" Mum looked serious, as though she was now coming to the same conclusion as me, that this was more than simply a case of mixed-up holiday dates.

"I didn't, but I'm starting to think it's possible. I'll see if I can come up with some leads tomorrow. Don't worry. I'll do my best." Pete had already got back to me with the details of a contact in Birmingham who'd be able to bypass the code on Bea's phone, so that was my priority.

"But you said yourself, she's not a painting and that's what you're normally looking for."

"It should be simpler to track down Bea." I pointed out. "In theory anyway. Paintings are easier to steal, easier to transport, easier to dispose of. Far easier than people, probably. And in some ways, there are a lot of similarities. Whether it's Bea or stolen art, I'm just seeing what the fragments left behind can tell me. But let's hope these women tonight have something because at the moment I don't have many fragments." I grabbed my bag and kissed her cheek. "Don't wait up."

"So, spill." Anna got into the car and looked at me expectantly. I started the engine and put it in gear. "Hang on. You haven't replied to my messages today. Tell me about Pete."

"What do you want to know?" I asked, wishing I hadn't made that flip comment about him earlier. "He's a bit over six foot, well built, fair hair, hazel eyes. Former Special Forces, he now provides security services in the private sector. Currently, he and his team are looking after an American news crew in Syria. Divorced, two children. Ex-wife moved to Australia with the kids when she remarried. He sees them as often as he can. His favourite author is John le Carre—somewhat predictable but there you go. He has a lovely cottage in Cornwall where he'd like to spend more time, ideally with me. Drives a black Audi. This one, in fact; I borrowed it. Great sense of humour, surprisingly good cook, terrible taste in music." I grinned at her. "So now you know. Shall we go?"

"I want to know what your relationship is with him. Not his online dating profile."

"I'm pretty sure he doesn't do online dating. I hope not, at any rate."

"And you and he have been an item for how long?"

"Did I say that we were an item?"

"You said—"

"I said I left him in my bed when I drove down here yesterday. You're the one placing a meaning on that." I smiled, teasing her.

"So—?"

"So, we've been seeing each other for a couple of years. We split up for a while, during which time I dated Kolya, and we picked up again about three months ago."

"That sounds like a relationship to me."

"I suppose it does. It's good and we're very happy."

"And you met two years ago?"

"Yes. The day after Chris was convicted to be precise."

"And how did it begin?"

"You ask a lot of questions, Anna." I put my hand back on the gearstick but she gave me a warning look and I didn't dare drive off.

"I'm your sister. It's my job."

"Okay. I'd chased a painting all over Europe and finally tracked it to Belarus. The gang holding it were dodgier than most, so someone put me in touch with Pete and he and his team came along as protection. We spent two days hanging around a derelict factory, waiting and talking and so on and all the time there was this growing attraction, I suppose."

"And?"

"And the van Gogh was dropped off. Pete's guys were watching in case of trouble. I checked the painting and when I was happy, the delivery man was given part payment and told the balance would be transferred once we were safely out of the country, then he was sent on his way."

"And you started dating after that?"

"Not exactly, although we had agreed that we'd like to have dinner sometime, get to know each other in a setting where we didn't need body armour. But it was a buzz, lots of adrenaline and we were driving back to the hotel and Pete just whispered in my ear. And that was that. We had some time to kill before we left for our flight and, well, you know how it is."

"No, I don't know how it is. I started seeing Olly at med school after our eyes met across the cadaver we were dissecting. No adrenaline and adventure to speak of. What did he whisper?"

"I'm not telling you, it was rude. But it was exactly how I felt too." I put the car in gear and moved away from the kerb. "And here we are, two years later, bar a break for a few months, and it's great fun and I'm very happy with how things are." I hoped that would be an end to this conversation.

"So why hide him away?" Anna obviously wasn't going to let it drop.

"I don't think I am. But you know what Mum's like. She'll be trying to get us down the aisle. There's no need whatsoever for her to know about Pete. Not yet, at any rate."

"Do you have a photo of him?" Anna picked up my phone and waved it in front of my face to unlock it.

"There's an album called Maldives." I sighed; it was easier to tell her everything.

"You were with him in the Maldives at Christmas? I thought you went with friends?"

"Friend. Singular. I don't think I said who I was with, did I?"

"No. Now you come to mention it, you were very vague." Anna began swiping through the photos and from the corner of my eye I glimpsed azure seas, cloudless skies, crumpled linen, sun-bleached decking. Quite a contrast from the drizzle outside. "Crikey."

"What?" I stopped at the lights and looked at the image on the screen, alarmed for a moment that it might be a picture I'd rather she didn't see, but it was just one I'd taken of Pete waking up beside me, all messy hair, sleepy smile and tanned, bare chest. I relaxed and smiled. "Yes, it's a nice photo."

"I can see why you couldn't keep your hands off him."

"When we first got together it wasn't in a posh cabin on stilts over the water like that. It was a crappy hotel with musty bedlinen and we'd been on a stakeout for two days."

"Did you care?"

"Not in the slightest. If anything, that made it hotter. You know, all raw and passionate." I grinned at her, remembering. "Although I must say, on the whole, I do prefer linen sheets and an ocean breeze."

"I can imagine. Still, it's nice to know you have a boyfriend. Of sorts. Can I meet him?"

"Nope." I pulled into a parking space outside the bar. "We don't do meeting each other's families. Maybe when we know where this is going."

"I'd just like to see him in the flesh." Anna continued swiping through pictures. She paused on one of Pete walking out of the waves towards me. "How old is he?"

"Thirty-nine."

"Olly's younger. He doesn't have a body like Pete's. I should show him these; that would get him to the gym more often."

"That's because Olly's an A&E consultant. Pete's effectively still a soldier. It's a job with very different requirements, Anna." I took the keys from the ignition and snatched my phone from her. "Now, you need to concentrate this evening. And not on my sex life. I have to find out who Bea was friendly with, who she might have told about this bloke she was seeing. I'm not sure either of these women were especially close to her anymore but they may know something."

"What do you know so far?"

"Actual cold, hard facts?" I sighed. "I know that Bea was keeping secrets. Nothing more. Absolutely sod all, to be honest."

12

The Cannonball was a basement bar where my crowd had done a lot of our teenage drinking, and over a decade later it had barely changed; the corner bar with its polished mahogany top and curving brass rail was still there, the brick vaulted ceiling was the same and I had no doubt the ladies' loo would be as shabby as ever.

What had altered—aside from the absence of a fug of cigarette smoke—was the clientele. It seemed the place was no longer popular with young people. Instead, the tables were dotted with couples and small groups of women, a couple of men on their own scrolling down their phones at either end of the bar.

I saw the two women we were there to meet, Susie and Joanna, before they saw me. Anna and I went over and I rearranged my face from stressed-friend-of-missing-woman to gosh-meeting-up-after-all-these-years-is-such-fun. There were kisses on cheeks, rhetorical assertions that we all looked just the same, and the surreptitious sizing-up of each other, noticing how we really had changed.

The pair of them clocked everything about my appearance from the absence of a wedding band, to the diamonds in my ears, the Mulberry bag over my shoulder, the boots on my feet, the tiny wrinkles at the corners of my eyes.

And I noticed them. Partly from habit, because observing minute details was a large part of how I made a living and partly because I wasn't immune from that kind of competition either.

I hadn't chosen these women to join us because we'd been close at school. No, I'd invited them because they'd been the popular girls, the ones who'd known everything that was going on and who didn't miss a thing if it could bolster their egos or cut you down to size, whether that was the boyfriend they wanted to steal or you looking better than them in your new jeans.

After school, we'd lost touch but the advent of Facebook and the like enabled them to exercise their teenage tendencies again. So, they "friended" everyone they remembered to widen the audience to whom they could show off their well-paid husbands, Joules-clad children, and *#makingmemories* holidays.

I had no idea who Bea was in contact with now and her avoidance of social media meant that I had no convenient list of friends to mine. But these women had been the Queen Bees fifteen years ago and I was willing to bet that they still knew every bit of gossip going.

I headed for the bar, ordered soda and lime for me and Pinot Noir for Anna and while the bartender got my change, I noticed one of the lone drinkers eyeing me up, not especially discreetly.

"Haven't I seen you in here before?" In his early thirties, he wore a good suit that needed pressing and there was a faint mark on his finger where his wedding ring had been. He had the entitled air of a man who used to have his pick of girls but who was having trouble dealing with grown women now that his marriage had failed. Failed pretty recently, I guessed.

"Not for a long time. I'm just in town catching up with family and friends." I smiled politely, took my change and picked up my drinks.

"We've definitely met before. You were younger."

"I daresay you were too. You were probably a regular here when I was, about fifteen years ago. A long time."

He looked me up and down again, assessing whether I was worth pursuing. The expression on my face made it clear that I wasn't. I returned to the table aware of his eyes on my back.

"Do you know Patrick?" Joanna Wilson flicked a glance in the direction of the man at the bar. In her heyday, she'd had the straightest, shiniest blonde hair and the haughtiest manner, the leader of the in-crowd, always the first with new clothes or make-up. Now, she wore the same jeans and dressy top that seemed to be the uniform of the yummy mummy on a night out.

"He seems vaguely familiar." I took a seat opposite her on one of the old pews that still lined the walls.

"He was in the same year as us. At St Eldred's." The boys' school next door to ours had been a source of fascination once we hit our teens. Boys we'd never even noticed before suddenly had potential and at an all-girl school, a boyfriend was status, no matter how nerdy he might be.

"Did he marry someone we know?"

"A girl from Cheltenham, I think. She left him a while ago when he had an affair. I haven't spoken to him in years."

Her animosity obviously dated back to our schooldays. Had he spurned her attentions all those years ago, I wondered?

"Now he's in here most nights as far as I know, chatting up anything with a pulse." Susie Jeffries leant in as she spoke, her tone equally dismissive, following the leader just as she'd done as Joanna's loyal lieutenant all those years ago. "Will knows him a little. He says that if he concentrated on his job he'd be successful, but he prefers to chase women and drink too much."

I wasn't keen on being described as 'anything with a pulse' but then, Joanna and Susie had never been my friends. I hadn't been cool with my black clothes and my tendency to visit art galleries and read too many books. Bea had been though, and these two, who were happy to bestow their friendship on her, had seen me as a plus-one to be tolerated while they worked out why Bea bothered with me.

The conversation drifted along for a while, the pair of them grilling me about my life. Anna was less interesting to them; a couple of years older, professionally successful, happily married to a well-paid husband; there was no way of undermining her. With me, on the other hand, they were like sharks scenting for that drop of blood in the ocean, looking for a vulnerability to pick apart. Not that I was going to reveal one.

"Kate, you never post much about your job on Facebook. What is it exactly that you do? A gallery or something, isn't it?"

"I'm an art consultant. My clients are organisations and individuals who want my advice in order to develop their collections. And I do some security consulting." That was my stock answer and it was dull enough to shut down a conversational tack pretty quickly. Except when someone like Joanna saw an opportunity to patronise me.

"How interesting. It must be lovely to spend all day choosing pictures for people. And the security thing, is that burglar alarms?"

"Not really. I work with insurance companies, galleries, owners and so on to recover stolen artworks."

"Kate's job is very exciting. She's always travelling to amazing places and she works with some very interesting people." Anna butted in, obviously not appreciating Joanna's tone. "Billionaires and all sorts."

"How fascinating. Anyone we'd have heard of?" Sharp-eyed and curious, I could see Joanna wondering how someone she'd previously dismissed as dull and nerdy ended up mingling with the super-rich.

"Almost certainly, but there are confidentiality agreements on both sides. It's all very discreet." I kicked Anna and smiled blandly, ever the professional, and the pair of them did the same, faking understanding but clearly itching to know more.

"I do enjoy seeing your pictures of the places you've been to." Susie's voice still had the breathy quality she'd affected as a teenager. "Your Christmas trip looked lovely. The Seychelles wasn't it?"

"The Maldives. It was perfect. I learnt to dive and saw manta rays up close. I'd love to return someday."

"And who did you go with?" I could see her ready to pity me now, poor childless Kate holidaying alone.

"A guy I'm seeing. We met through work. He's also in the security business, but he doesn't have anything to do with burglar alarms either."

I saw Anna glance at me curiously, wondering why I was willing to mention Pete to these women but kept so tight-lipped about him otherwise. It worked though; Susie and Joanna latched onto that and grilled me a little and I dropped a few inconsequential details to keep them interested but it encouraged more talk of relationships.

Although they patronised me for not having a ring on my finger, their own marriages sounded pretty shaky and I guessed that Susie's drinking—her glass was soon empty and she looked fidgety—was linked to the rather brittle way she talked about her husband, Will. I wondered whether the flirting with his secretary that she joked about might have got out of hand.

Joanna didn't say much about her marriage beyond making sure that we were suitably impressed by her husband's job as an actuary in Birmingham and some complaints about the long hours he worked. Although patronising about my spinster status, she seemed tense and on edge and I got the impression that she was bored as a stay-at-home mother with a largely absent husband, Alastair. At school, she'd been intolerant of negligent boyfriends and unless leopards could change their spots, I thought Alastair would do well to pay more attention before her eye wandered.

Although both Joanna and Susie stressed how perfect their marriages were, the looks in their eyes rather gave the lie to their words. Before someone felt the need to start making confessions, I moved the conversation on.

"I hoped to catch up with Beatrice while I'm in town but it seems she's away on holiday. Hopefully somewhere warmer than here." I paused, waiting for one of them to pass comment and praying that they would have some nugget that would make this evening worth my while.

"You know, I don't see her around very often," Joanna spoke briskly. "I bump into her occasionally when I'm in town shopping but that's about it."

"I saw Bea a few months ago, a week or two before Christmas," Susie said. "It was in that place on Friar Street that we all used to go to on our birthdays. Then it became a Thai restaurant. Anyway, it's changed hands again and I was there with Will and Bea was at a table in the corner."

"Who was she with?" I asked, ears pricking up.

"I couldn't tell you. A man, but I didn't get a clear view of him. She came over to say hello and I remember that she was very bubbly and excited, so I think it must have been a date, but I don't know what he looked like. For all I know, he could be a dead ringer for Quasimodo."

"Well, they say there's no accounting for taste." I smiled. "She didn't mention that they were intending to go away on holiday or anything?"

"No. We just talked about plans for Christmas. She was going to spend it with her mother, I think." Susie looked thoughtful, as though there was something on the edge of her consciousness but nothing took shape.

"I wonder where she's gone." I shrugged, taking care to keep my tone light. "It seems weird that she's not answering her phone or emails."

"She probably wants some peace and quiet." Joanna was snappy and I raised an eyebrow. Then more calmly, with a sweet smile, "You know, perhaps she feels that she needs to get away and reflect on things for a bit. I'm sure she'll call you back soon."

"Possibly. I wish I'd been able to give her some notice that I was coming down. It's been a while since we caught up," I said evenly, shrugging, although I wondered what Bea had done to provoke Joanna's attitude.

I didn't want to ask more questions, so I moved the conversation on to their holidays and heard about Joanna's planned Easter trip to Ibiza where they would, naturally, be staying in the quiet part of the island, the 'real' Ibiza, with not a stag party in sight. Susie and her family were off to Devon, scoring high on the middle-class brag-o-meter for having their own cottage there, not booking a rental.

"Are you going anywhere nice, Kate? With Steve, wasn't it?" Joanna asked, probably looking for somewhere new to aim a barb.

"Pete. And no, we've made no plans yet. If he's in the country, then we might go down to his place in Cornwall. If not, I'd like to catch up with one of my West Coast clients. He keeps inviting me to his house in Big Sur so I may take him up on that and spend a couple of days watching whales from his deck." I smiled. "All a bit vague, really."

"How very glamorous." Joanna's tone was sharp and I realised that I'd overstepped the mark. I was allowed to talk about my life as long as I made it sound like a poor shadow of a thing next to their Boden catalogue lifestyles. I hadn't been bragging, but I obviously hadn't given the impression of wishing that I could trade my trips for buckets and spades with small children.

Enough, I thought. I'd learnt a few things; that no-one knew who Beatrice was close to these days, that she'd been pretty secretive about her lover and not only with me and Caroline, and that I was very glad I hadn't stayed in my home town, married a solicitor and had a load of kids.

Not long after, Anna and I made our excuses, blaming her early start and my jet lag. Before we left, I popped to the Ladies. As I'd expected, it was just as grotty as a decade or so earlier. Susie was already in there, her handbag balanced on the basin as she rummaged through it, a little agitated.

"Everything okay?" I asked, squinting into the mirror and pretending to fish an eyelash out of my eye.

"Yes. I've just got a headache and want a painkiller. Here they are." Via the mirror, I saw her pull a box out of her bag, hurriedly push a couple out of the blister pack and slug them down with water from a small Evian bottle. "I need the loo and I bet there's no hook. Can you watch my bag for me?"

"Of course." I continued tidying myself up, but once I heard the cubicle door lock, I flicked open the flap of Susie's handbag to look at the pill box, making a mental note of the name. Hearing no rustle of paper or flush, I picked up the Evian bottle. I sniffed the contents; nothing. Then I took a sip; vodka. Interesting.

ANNA AND I LEFT, walking slowly back to my car, and I reflected on what I'd learnt. It wasn't much but there were a couple more crumbs of information that might prove useful. The restaurant where Susie had seen Bea and a mystery man, another visit to the Cannonball to see if the bartender recognised Bea's photograph, maybe Patrick too, if I could catch him sober. And Joanna had clearly had some sort of falling-out with Beatrice, however minor, and I thought I'd follow that up in a day or two. Susie too, for that matter, in case something came to mind, floating in on a tide of vodka by the look of it.

"Anna, why would you prescribe oxycodone?"

"Serious pain. It's an opiate, pretty heavy-duty stuff. Addictive if you're not careful. Why do you ask?"

"Susie had a pack in her bag. In the loo, she was swigging them down two at a time with vodka."

"That's not good. And quite a cocktail on top of the wine she was putting away." Anna pulled a face. "Is it relevant to Bea, do you think?"

"Probably not. But worth knowing, perhaps." I unlocked the car and we got in. "All that effort put into making their lives appear perfect and neither of them are happy. If they hadn't been so vile at school, I'd feel sorry for them."

13

After a restless night with little sleep, I was out for a run before dawn, extending my route to seven or eight miles as I worked out my plan for the day. Ten minutes or so from home and the cup of tea I was looking forward to, my phone vibrated in my pocket. Pete.

"Morning." I slowed to a walk. "How's it going?"

"Okay. Digs are a bit grotty but no-one's shooting at us right now, so that's good." Pete was always unremittingly positive when he phoned home, years of practice from his Army days, I supposed. "Did you get my message about Ben?"

"Yes, I'm off to Birmingham to see him this afternoon. Fingers crossed he'll be able to unlock the phone."

"I'm sure he will. How was your evening? Useful?"

"Maybe. It gave me a couple of things to follow up. Mostly it was a bit depressing."

"Tell me. I need to be distracted from the fact that something bit me while I was asleep." Despite his words, I could hear the smile in his voice.

"The women we met. One is drinking too much and

slugging down painkillers, the other is so tightly wound, it's as though she's ready to explode. At school, they seemed destined to have such perfect lives and now they're so unhappy."

"Did you tell them how happy you are? And how I'm the best boyfriend in the world?"

"Pretty much. I rather enjoyed ensuring they knew exactly how great my life is. And I'm looking forward to getting back to that life. But first, I'm off to the glamour of Birmingham city centre."

I WASN'T sure what I expected Ben Trevelyan's operation to look like. I half-expected it to be painfully corporate but equally, I wouldn't have been surprised if he was wearing a stained Nirvana t-shirt and operating out of his mother's basement. In fact, his office was in a converted marmalade factory in Digbeth on the edge of the city centre, in a neighbourhood where it was impossible to move for vintage trainer shops, craft beer bars, and skateboard emporia. Millennial central. I had a sinking feeling my saviour was going to turn out to be about twenty.

After she'd called his office and I'd signed in, I followed the receptionist's directions and found Ben in an open plan space upstairs, waiting for me by the table football. Rather than the geeky almost-teenager I expected, instead Ben was in his early thirties with short dark hair, brown eyes, and more confidence and social skills than I was used to in my tech guys.

"Hi, Kate." He reached out to shake my hand. "Pete said you needed to get into a smartphone?"

"Yes, it's here. Thanks for this."

Despite the casual vibe of the shared office space with its

trendy sofas, coffee machines, and hammock, I noticed that his door had a biometric lock. So, he was a hacker, but a careful, security-conscious hacker. He was also the only other person here apart from me who wasn't wearing a hoodie. Multiple desks in the room were stacked with bits of hardware and he turned the phone over in his hand as I explained why we were worried about Bea.

"This shouldn't take long. The security on this model was nothing to write home about. The thing is, normally I'm looking into corporate issues and so on." Ben looked a little wary. "This is a personal phone; you might find things on here that are unexpected, upsetting even. I wouldn't usually do this for a private individual but Pete told me how important it was."

"It's okay, nothing you find will surprise me. Besides, it's all I've got. Missing people aren't my usual area."

"Stolen pictures usually, isn't it?"

"That's right. Pete and his team look after me if I have to go somewhere dodgy to pick up a painting. He'll tell you that I'm not easily shocked." I smiled, reassuring. "I just need to find Bea."

"I see. What do you think might have happened?"

"I have no idea. Everyone thought she was on holiday but it's been too long now. This phone was in her bedside drawer and it's not her usual one, according to her mother. She was hiding something and whatever it was, I reckon it's on there."

"A lover?"

"There's a man in the picture somewhere, for sure. But she didn't tell me or her mother about him so it's someone she wanted to keep quiet. I'm hoping that if I can match up what's on there with a rather cryptic diary then I might be able to work out where they were meeting and get a lead that way. So far, the only thing we've come up with is Pete's suggestion that she was working as an escort."

"Not impossible." Ben shrugged.

"But not likely, I don't think. We'll see though, when you've worked your magic." I smiled, expectant, waiting for him to stop being sympathetic and crack on. His concern for my delicate sensibilities was appreciated but I had a to-do list for today and didn't want to waste time on more conversation than was strictly necessary.

Ben got the message and sat down at a computer behind him. After a couple of minutes of logging into screens, he connected a cord to the phone and turned back to me.

"It'll take up to half an hour to run through everything. Fancy a coffee?"

While he fiddled with pods and a machine, I looked around his office. I didn't know a lot of private investigators, my work being quite specialist. The ones I did use were successful but I always imagined most of them based in seedy offices above backstreet bookmakers rather than places like this, never making any money because they pursued truth and justice regardless of remuneration. Maybe I'd read too much crime fiction. People had in the past suggested I branch out in that direction, but I preferred artwork and was too well paid to give that up. Truth and justice were wonderful ideals but they wouldn't support my shoe habit like missing Cézannes.

"How do you know Pete?" I asked, taking my cup from Ben.

"In my previous role, I worked in military intelligence. Since I set up on my own, I freelance in the same sort of work. Much as Pete does."

"Pete's a mercenary, however you dress it up." I smiled,

this being a discussion he and I had many times. It was a matter of semantics.

"Aren't we all? You too?" Ben grinned. "We all sell our skills and our services, and we pick and choose who we work for. If we're good, we get to be pickier. You know how fussy Pete is. And unlike when he was a soldier, he doesn't get involved in anything he objects to. We all operate within our own moral codes. What are your boundaries?"

"No mafia, no turf wars, no war criminals, no obvious psychopaths. And I pass on the jobs that don't interest me or where people think they can get away with paying me peanuts. I'm very picky too."

"And we can determine how and when we work, which is nice. Hence Christmas in the Maldives. That was where you and Pete went, wasn't it?"

"It sounds as though he's told you quite a bit about me."

"Not really, he's very discreet. But I know he thinks a lot of you." Ben's gaze was assessing and I got the feeling that I was being analysed along with Bea's mobile.

"So he should." I smiled and changed the subject. "How's that passcode coming on?"

Ben spun round in his chair, back to the computer the phone was hooked up to, tapped a few keys and disconnected everything.

"All done. What's your email address? I'll send you the messages. And—" he paused, swiping through the phone. "I'd keep this locked. You probably won't want Beatrice's mother going through it." He wrote a six-digit number on a business card and slid it and the mobile to me. Unable to wait, I picked it up and opened the texts. All of them were between Beatrice and someone called J. The final one from J said simply:

"8 p.m. Don't be late."

The reply from Bea just said:

"OK."

They were dated the day before she was last seen.

I scrolled back. There were hundreds of texts, stretching back months. Photos sent by Bea, none from the mysterious J. I looked up at Ben.

"They're all downloaded. I'll sort them in date order when I send them if that helps. Easier to go through them and build up a pattern. Does the last one tell you anything at first glance?"

"No. It looks as if they're all between Bea and the same person, though. So she's probably not working as an escort."

"That's something. Do the photos give you any clues?"

"I don't know if I dare look." But I needed to. There were a hundred or so in an unnamed album, nothing that looked useful at first glance, no handy full-face shot of a man who might be J. Countryside, hills, a few city snapshots, a few with other people in restaurants, swish hotel rooms, and a number she certainly wouldn't want her mother to see. I guessed she'd be uncomfortable when she knew I'd seen them.

"And she's got no social media?" Ben sounded slightly incredulous.

"Nothing that I can find which makes it so much harder. Our digital footprints make it hard to disappear but if someone's always avoided that it probably makes it easier." I sighed, weary of one brick wall after another.

"You're probably right. Shall I try his number?" Ben suggested. "I can bounce it around. He won't know who's calling or where from."

"Go on then." The hairs on the back of my neck were prickling. This was information. This might lead me to her.

Imagine if J picked up or if Bea answered. Ben clicked some buttons and then cursed softly under his breath.

"Nothing. Number out of service. I'd guess it was a burner that's been disposed of." He started tapping on the keyboard in front of him. "I can't track its location either. That's all a bit worrying."

"That's a lot worrying." I corrected him. "He's been texting her frequently, they arrange to meet, then she goes missing and he gets rid of his phone. That doesn't seem the actions of a man with nothing to hide, does it?"

"I've put the number into a couple of databases. No record." Ben looked at me. "Anything in the browser history?" I checked. It was empty.

"The texts and images are it. There might be some details in the photos." I'd hoped for a nice big clue like an address or the name of a hotel and the date of a booking. This was going to be slow. Numbers and initials. I smiled at Ben and rummaged in my bag for a business card. "Thanks for your efforts. I appreciate it. My contact information is on that for your invoice."

"No charge. This is on me."

"Thanks, but it's okay." I smiled. "I don't work for strangers for free and I wouldn't expect other people to."

"As I said, I owe Pete a favour. Endless favours, to be honest. I wouldn't have made it back from Iraq without him." Ben came round from behind his desk and held out his hand. "I mean it. If there's anything else you want me to check out, just let me know. I drew a blank with that number, but you'd be amazed what else I can find. Usually. The system will have copied the photos. Would you like me to look at them? Not the more personal ones, obviously. And it's really the data, geo-tagging and so on, not the pictures themselves." He looked a bit awkward, as though I might have thought he was planning to leer at Bea's more intimate pictures.

"It's fine. If you have time, that would be very helpful."

DRIVING AWAY, I felt a weight settle on my shoulders, the optimism of my journey having already evaporated. I'd been hoping for an answer, that the phone would give me enough information that I could track Bea down this afternoon. All I knew was that her lover had the initial J. And if she was working as an escort, then she wasn't a very busy one. It was a start, but certainly not enough that I could reassure Caroline and flee back up to Scotland.

And I was more worried. Those last couple of messages were curt; J and Beatrice didn't sound like people planning a romantic meeting. How had that relationship begun, how had it changed, and how had it ended? If it had ended. Maybe they were blissfully happy in some paradise somewhere with fake identities.

This afternoon and tomorrow, I would have to read every single one of those texts. Unless I got lucky, finding Beatrice was going to be as slow a process as hunting a looted painting—hours of work piecing together tiny scraps of information to see if I could build up a picture of Bea's life and what had happened.

14

When I got back from Birmingham I spent hours skimming through the hundreds of texts between Bea and J, hoping for an obvious starting point but there was nothing that I could see.

About midnight, knowing I would need to pick apart the more cryptic texts to find a clue to follow and that I was too weary to make sense of them, I gave up and went to bed although I slept fitfully and was up early in the morning.

As well as my code-breaking, I needed to try to get a handle on the nature of Bea's relationship with J and how it had gone from the hearts and flowers of the first few texts, to the brief words of the last. There was a definite hardening in the tone of J's messages and I wondered what had precipitated that.

I hoped that studying the pictures might prove fruitful, maybe I could identify a location. Finding Beatrice might be hard, but J was another avenue to explore. Perhaps he didn't keep his life as obsessively private as Bea. Maybe those other people in the photographs would give me a lead—Bea and her mystery man had obviously socialised together. Maybe J was the loose thread that would unravel everything when I pulled at it. I hoped so, at any rate.

After a run to wake myself up, I showered, dressed, grabbed a cuppa, and settled down at the dining room table with my laptop, Ben's printouts of the texts, and Bea's phone.

I read the messages first, noting down any dates and times and places mentioned. No names were given in full, but I'd go back to them later as I was pretty sure that a lot were pubs and restaurants. A few hotels too, with gushing comments as to how excited one or both of them—usually Bea—was to be spending the whole night together. Those last ones generally tallied with a pic of Bea showing what delights from the naughty knicker drawer J could look forward to when he arrived.

I'm not a prude by a long stretch, but seeing my oldest friend behaving like this, and with a man who didn't attempt to hide the fact that he was married, made me uncomfortable. He made all the usual excuses in his texts—that his wife didn't understand him, that they'd got married too young, even that she was mentally unstable and he couldn't risk leaving her now, and so on. The justifications that I'd have expected someone naive and inexperienced to have fallen for, not Beatrice who was a grown woman and should have seen straight through them.

The change in tone happened about six weeks or so before Bea was last seen. I was reading between the lines to a degree, but it seemed that Beatrice had decided that she was no longer satisfied to be his bit on the side and had started trying to pin J down as to exactly when he planned to leave his wife, only ever referred to as A. J's manner changed quite sharply from romantic nothings to a sharp:

"We've talked about this. It's not possible. Don't let's go through it again."

After that, Bea sounded a little apologetic, they arranged a tryst, and then there was a gap for a few days. That was surprising; they usually messaged half a dozen or more times each day, I'd ploughed through hundreds and hundreds of their inanities. The next message was from Beatrice and decidedly conciliatory in tone:

"I'm so sorry I was unreasonable. I know you're right. You have to wait for a suitable moment to leave her. Let's meet up tonight."

J didn't reply straightaway, which was unusual, but waited several hours. Then:

"Okay. 8 at the P Ho."

There had obviously been an argument, enough for both to back off for a few days. Had the silence been a stand-off? Both seeing who would crumble first—whether that was J realising that Bea was serious or Bea swallowing her pride and deciding that a part-time J was better than no J? It surprised me that Beatrice was willing to put up with that. I wouldn't have expected her to settle for being anyone's second-best.

And then, with Bea having shown her weakness, the warmth faded from J's texts. Instead of his seductive suggestions for a rendezvous they became more cursory:

"I'll meet you at your place around nine but I need to be home by midnight so we'll have to be quick."

I raised my eyebrows. So romantic.

J also seemed more controlling too, in a way that I recognised all too well from my relationship with Chris. J would demand to know where she'd been, who with, why she hadn't been at home when he'd called. He would accuse her of flirting with a waiter or barman, ask her whether she'd dated or slept with them in the past.

When I'd been seeing Chris, it had followed a similar pattern. After a while, instead of courting me, he wanted to own me. He felt I should account for my time, that I should be available whenever it suited him. The romance faded, the warmth and the tenderness, and I was left in a relationship with someone who both refused to let me go but didn't seem to like me very much.

It had come to a head when a flight was delayed by bad weather. I called Chris from the departure lounge to tell him that I was going to have to skip dinner that night. He'd become enraged, ranting and yelling as he accused me of inventing this freak storm as a way of covering up that I was with another man. I remembered listening to his outburst, afraid and upset and knowing that I would have to end this when I saw him next.

Despite my attempts to word it in as calm and self-effacing manner as possible, 'it's not you, it's me' and all that, Chris lost it. He punched me, blacking my eye and cracking my cheekbone, slapped me, and yanked me back by my hair when I tried to run. When I fell to the ground, I remembered him kicking me in the ribs, then his hand on my throat, a blur of pain and panic. When I came to, shaking and disoriented, all I felt was relief that he'd gone.

The texts between J and Beatrice reminded me of the end-stages of my relationship, and reading them I had the same tight fear in the pit of my stomach that I'd felt when Chris messaged me. By the time I got to the most recent ones, where he was curt and Bea was submissive, I was almost holding my breath, afraid to see where this toxic affair had ended up.

But there was no end. As I'd seen in Ben's office the last messages were simply:

"8 p.m. Don't be late."

And Bea's:

"OK."

No more, nothing approaching a clue as to where Bea might be. Not even the initials of where they were meeting.

I wandered through to the kitchen and made more tea, leaning on the draining board for a while as I watched Dad digging the veg patch. I didn't need to ask whether he wanted a cuppa.

"Here you go." I held out the mug and he straightened up.

"Thanks love."

"Planting potatoes?" I asked, that being about the extent of my vegetable-growing knowledge.

"Not for a bit, but soon, if it stays nice. How are you getting on?"

"Just reading the stuff we pulled off Bea's phone yesterday. Text messages and so on. Lots of words but no real information."

"So what's your next step?"

"I'm going to look at the photos, see whether there's anything in them to tell me where they were taken and so on. Maybe that will give me some locations to check out. And I'll carry on trying to decipher pub and hotel names from initials."

"No big clues then?"

"No. Only tiny ones."

"They make it seem easy on the telly." Dad took a swig of tea.

"Don't they just? Mind you, they have tech that I don't.

And it's not as though I'm exactly qualified to do this, Dad. I'm worried I'm missing something obvious."

"Kate, love, people pay you to go out and track down their paintings that are worth a fortune. You must have a nose for it or they wouldn't trust you." He shrugged, leaning on his spade. It was a reasonable point.

Back in the dining room, I considered my list of dates and places of Bea and J's assignations, and combining it with the contents of Bea's diary I started to decipher some of them, searching my memory and the internet. Some were more informative, even the odd postcode, presumably for sat-nav or maps, and before long I had a shortlist of pubs and hotels in the area between Worcester and Birmingham —Stourbridge, Kidderminster, Droitwich—nowhere too far away.

I opened my email and found a message from Ben. Helpfully, he'd compiled some of the images in Bea's photographs into a gallery of men's faces so that I'd have something to show to people. I could have hugged him for saving me a job.

But he'd also discovered a piece of information that excited me. Some of the photos on Bea's phone had been taken at her house on the dates she'd sent them, so nothing useful there. And most of the rest had no geotags on them, but there were a few from roughly the same location. He'd checked the grid reference and it was in Birmingham, the suburb of Edgbaston to be precise. He wasn't sure exactly which property it was, but I'd got a limited number of possible options to work with.

Going back to my list of places, I found one that looked likely: B15 7TB and a number that surely had to be a house number. 27 Albert Road. I searched online and bingo—it had been up for sale recently. It was marked as under offer but according to the Land Registry, the transaction hadn't yet been concluded. No details regarding ownership but I was sure I could fill those gaps in later.

I was grinning, virtually high-fiving myself as I sent a grateful email to Ben. I'd got some pubs to call at with a photo of Bea and possibly the elusive J. And I had an address to scope out. That was this afternoon sorted.

15

By now, my neck was aching and my eyes were gritty from staring at screens. After going through all the pictures and text messages, some of which had undoubtedly affected my opinion of my oldest friend, and not necessarily for the better, however much I tried not to judge, I was keen to get out of the house.

I bolted a bowl of cereal and saved the most useful images into an album on my mobile. Closing everything down, I took care not to leave the passcode for Bea's phone lying around in case Mum saw it and decided to help me. Well-meaning she was, I didn't want her seeing some of those photos.

"Where are we starting?"

"We?" I looked up as I was tying my bootlaces to find Mum in the hallway, holding her jacket, handbag over her shoulder. Feeling positive for the first time since going to Worcester, I'd told Mum and Dad that I was off on a road trip, but I didn't remember asking for a road-trip buddy.

"I thought I'd come too. It might be helpful to have

company. A partner. You know, how you work with Pete sometimes."

"Why? In case of trouble? With the best will in the world, Mum, you're no-one's idea of back-up. And Pete's not my partner. I take him with me because he—" I stopped. She didn't need to know why Pete was useful to have around at times.

"And we can have a nice chat while you're driving. You've been so busy looking for Beatrice and we must have lots to catch up on." She buttoned her navy Jaeger jacket and looked at me expectantly, more WI than MI6. I smiled instead of sighing, grabbed my keys and bag and off we set.

First stop was the Pack Horse in Droitwich. I was pretty sure that this was where Bea and J had met one evening in November when all was still hearts and flowers, him likening her red hair to a sunset and Bea telling him how handsome he was. She'd also sent him a picture where he replied with some comment about her being a natural redhead, but I preferred to skip over that. If I was right, they'd been there a few times, hopefully improving my chances of finding a member of staff who'd recognise her.

"I'll go in. Mum, can you wait here? I'll only be ten minutes or so and we've a fair amount of ground to cover this afternoon." She tutted a little, suggested nipping to the nearby Waitrose and then pulled a book from her bag and told me that she didn't want to be a bother. I smiled and was proud of myself for not rolling my eyes. Truly, staying with my parents seemed to make me regress to being a teenager.

The pub was a half-timbered Tudor building, much older than most of those around it and with the sloping walls and low lintels of its type. No longer the old-fashioned boozer I vaguely remembered, the staff were all in white shirts and long black aprons and it had been stripped of its nicotine-stained woodchip wallpaper. Now it was all cream paint, old oak tables, and wood burning stoves in the inglenook fireplaces. It looked a cosy place to spend a winter's evening and I could imagine Bea there.

At two in the afternoon, the lunchtime trade was easing off and the staff were winding down, catching up with washing glasses and wiping tables. I hitched a hip onto a barstool and ordered a lemonade.

"If you've got a minute," I began as I was handed my change by the bartender. "I'm looking for someone. An old friend seems to have taken off without telling anyone and her family is worried." I'd thought about making something up but creating a fiction could cause problems later. I preferred to save the lying through my teeth for when I really needed it.

"Sure." The young woman smiled. "Is she a regular?"

"I'm not sure, but I think she's been in a few times." I pulled up a picture of Bea on my phone. "This is fairly recent. She would have been with a man, probably just the two of them."

"Maybe. She looks vaguely familiar but—" She shrugged and I flicked to pictures of the three men on my shortlist.

"I think she would have been with one of these men."

"I've seen him before." She pointed to a man with fair hair and striking cheekbones. "You tend to remember the good-looking ones, don't you?"

"Absolutely." I looked again at the picture. It wasn't a brilliant photo and given the angle it was taken, I couldn't see what colour his eyes were. He was also wearing a dinner jacket so nothing unique or distinctive there. But yes, handsome enough in a somewhat generic way. "I don't suppose you can remember anything else about them? You know, how they acted around each other, something you overheard, that sort of thing?"

"I'm sorry. But I'm pretty sure they were here together, if that's any help. Not in the last few weeks though. Maybe a month ago?"

"Do you have CCTV cameras?" It was a long shot.

"Just a burglar alarm at night, I'm afraid." The bartender looked regretful, sympathetic to my plight.

"Not to worry. You've been really helpful." I took a business card from my pocket and handed it to her. "If you think of anything else, anything at all, perhaps you'd let me know? Or if she comes in again?"

"No problem." She glanced at my card. "Art security consultant? Did she nick a Picasso before she went off?"

"No. I just want to find her and make sure she's okay. Thanks again."

"ANY JOY?" Mum replaced her bookmark and put the novel back in her bag as I got into the car.

"A bit. She vaguely recognised Bea but was more confident about one of the men in the photos. Nothing definite but at least it means I'm on the right track with working out what those initials meant in terms of a meeting place. So that's a start." I turned the ignition key. "Stourbridge next."

I fiddled with the sat-nav and set off, the traffic starting to get heavier with school-run mums in SUVs and people carriers. That reminded me, I needed to do some more digging into the woman who'd impersonated me at Bea's office. So far, the only idea I had on that front was pretty unlikely. Tomorrow, I'd call in again and see if Stacy had remembered any more or if she recognised any of those men.

"Are you busy at work at the moment?" Mum asked, clearly deciding it was time for the chat she'd threatened.

"Fairly."

"Can you afford to take time off to search for Bea?"

"Sort of. My consultancy clients all seem keen to extend their collections so I'm getting ready for the big spring sales. I could do with a day making phone calls and so on if I'm going to be here much longer. There's a looted Renoir I'm still on the trail of but that's turning into a marathon. And I'm working on a couple of recovery jobs. They're long-term though; nothing dramatic and they can wait. The police have either given up or arrested the thieves. My clients want the artwork returned but the cops aren't so bothered about that. Those jobs can wait until I'm home. If they get impatient then they can get someone else in."

"You don't want to lose business. Do you think they will go elsewhere?"

"No. I'm good at what I do. They know I'm more likely than most to get the pieces back in due course."

"And you work for the insurance companies?"

"Sometimes. Or the owners. They pay me a fee plus my expenses."

"Do you have a lot of expenses?" Mum seemed very interested in my job all of a sudden and I was getting wary.

"I might have to commission scientific reports, or to pay experts in a particular artist's techniques, or to travel long distances, or hire private investigators overseas, or sometimes I need additional security. That sort of thing. I use the best people for all those things and they don't come cheap."

"Security like Pete? Do you work with him often?"

"Every few months or so." Now I understood where she was going with this.

"You seem to know him well for someone you don't see that much of. And you've spoken to him a couple of times since you've been here. I gather from Anna that you sometimes bump into him when you're not working together."

"Uh-huh." I was non-committal, silently cursing Anna for her inability to keep information to herself. How much had she told Mum? And why had I told her anything in the first place?

"That's nice. You must have a lot in common."

I thought about that. Did we? On the face of it, we had next to nothing in common. While I was studying art history, he'd been in the Army, getting through the gruelling special forces selection process and then training to do heaven knows what.

While I built my career and made contacts in auction houses and galleries, he'd been in the world's trouble spots in life or death confrontations. He was a father of two and I didn't want children. I liked a glamorous party while he enjoyed a quieter social life. And yet I increasingly couldn't imagine not having him around. So what was it that drew us together? Maybe because we balanced each other?

"We have as much in common as we need to." That seemed a suitably innocuous answer. "He's excellent at his job and, when needed, that enables me to be very good at mine. And we have a similar sense of humour which helps when we have to spend long periods of time hanging around waiting for the bad guys to show up." I didn't think I'd given anything away there.

"And he's single?"

"Yes, Mum. His wife had an affair while he was in Iraq or somewhere like that. They got divorced and he came home from another deployment a year later to find she'd moved to Australia to get remarried and taken their two children with her."

"I see." Mum managed to convey a lot of judgement into those two words. An opinion I shared, if I was honest, although I was careful not to criticise Karen around Pete. He wouldn't have minded but it felt more diplomatic to say nothing. "What regiment was he in? And why did he leave the Army?"

I hesitated on both of those questions. Pete was discreet about the former and didn't like to talk about the latter. Fortunately, a roundabout hove into view for which I was very grateful.

"Look at the signs, Mum. I think I need the third exit here, don't I?"

16

The Plumber's Arms in Stourbridge was much like the Pack Horse; an old-fashioned drinkers' pub white-washed into gastropub uniformity in a bid to attract a younger crowd. A couple of the old-timers were playing cribbage at a table by the window, steadfastly resisting this modernisation.

I had a similar conversation with the barman in this pub, sipping some more lemonade as I did so. He recognised Beatrice but wasn't sure whether he'd seen any of the three men. Again, I left my card in case he remembered anything, assured him that no, she hadn't stolen a Rembrandt, and returned to Mum.

"Where to now?" She looked up from her book and I wondered if she was getting bored and we should head for home. But I wanted to check this address and I didn't ask her to come with me so I decided that she'd just have to put up with it.

"Edgbaston. I found a house there that Bea seems to have visited on several occasions according to the data that Ben got from the photos."

"How clever of him. It's a nice part of the city."

"Well yes, I suppose so." It was a middle-class suburb, popular with professionals and academics from the university. Latterly, it had become very expensive in a more flashy way as footballers and the like moved in. The streets were still tree-lined and the houses were genteel detached piles, but now more likely to have swimming pools and cinema rooms.

27 Albert Road was a large Edwardian house behind a wall with a fence on top, about seven or eight feet tall in total. There were new looking electric gates on the drive and a pedestrian gate with keypad entry.

I drove past a couple of times but couldn't see much so I parked round the corner and walked back. From what I could tell from the opposite side of the street, number 27 was newly painted, its stucco a tasteful off-white, and although streetlamps had started popping on around me, there didn't seem to be lights on inside. There was a burglar alarm box but no visible CCTV cameras.

The road was fairly busy for this time in the afternoon, on a route from a local school, I guessed. Taking my phone out, as though checking an address, I pressed the buzzer by the gate. No response. I tried a couple of four-digit codes – 1111, 1234 – hoping that one was the manufacturer's default and hadn't been changed, but none of them worked.

I carried on walking and checked out the properties on either side. After continuing to the corner—six houses down—and turning left, I turned left again and counted, trying to spot the rear elevation of number 27. I saw it; the same tasteful shade of stucco, but there were no lights on upstairs at the back either, despite the gathering dusk.

Returning to the front, I considered my options. The obvious thing to do, for me at any rate, was to find a way over the wall or to pick the lock on the smaller gate and take a look around. If someone was in, I could claim that it had been open and make up a fictitious name for whoever I claimed to be looking for. But I didn't have my tools with me and the road was too busy to risk climbing in, although I saw that there were enough trees and large shrubs on the verge to give me cover if I came back after dark.

That left the neighbours, then. Fortunately, neither were as security conscious as number 27 and the gates of their drives stood open. One house was completely dark with an empty driveway but the other had an enormous SUV and plenty of lights on. I walked briskly up the drive, trying to work out a cover story before deciding to wing it and see where that took me.

The woman who opened the door was about my age, hair in a ponytail, dressed in jeans and a sweatshirt. I couldn't tell how many kids were in the house but it sounded as though World War III had broken out in the background.

"Hi. I'm sorry to bother you but I'm trying to catch up with an acquaintance and for some reason the address I had written down was number 27. But I think I've made a mistake. Do you know who lives there?" I smiled, taking care to look a bit scatty. "I was scribbling it down at the same time as making sure the kids weren't killing each other. You know how it is."

"Don't I just?" The blonde woman grinned broadly, accepting me as a kindred spirit. "I'm afraid I have no idea who owns it at the moment. It's recently been sold, as far as I know."

"How annoying. My friend's an estate agent and she told me that she had the perfect house for me. I've looked at so many houses online that I probably wrote down this address by mistake. That's so frustrating, it looks exactly what we're after."

"You never know, it might come back on the market. It's been a while so the sale could have fallen through. You're looking to move here?"

"Yes, we're relocating from London and my husband really likes this neighbourhood." I tried to keep my left hand out of sight in case she spotted my ringless finger. "That's a real pity if it is sold. The schools here are supposed to be so good."

"They are. I don't know much about the house. The Richardsons lived there for a long time and then he died and she went to live with their son. A developer bought it. They've done masses of work—big kitchen extension, a swimming pool, a gym, dozens of builders and decorators."

"How lovely. Annoying if I've missed it. I wonder if my friend was the agent for this house? Beatrice Copley, petite, amazing red hair. I think she drives a silver Polo." I sounded casual, still working my yummy mummy persona.

"That sounds like her. She was here a lot, often in the evenings. Doing viewings I suppose."

"Must have been. Oh well, thanks for your help. I'll try to catch up with her and see if it's come back on the market."

"Do, it would be lovely to have another family next door."

I retraced my steps back to the road, thinking about this new information. It sounded as though this was somewhere Bea and J had met several times. Was he the owner, the architect, one of the tradesmen? It was a start.

At the other neighbour's house, lights were now on and a Volvo was parked in the drive. Time for a different tack, a different persona, and a different barefaced lie.

"Good afternoon," I began in my most brisk and efficient

tone as the door was opened by a sensible-looking lady of a certain age in a tweed skirt with a black Labrador standing beside her. "I wonder if you can help. My name's Jennifer Cameron, from the planning department. I'm making some investigations about number 27 next door and I hoped you might be able to answer a couple of questions please?"

"Goodness. Of course, I'll be happy to assist if I can." The *'Save Our Green Spaces'* sticker in the back window of the Volvo had indicated that she might not be keen on property developers and there was nothing people liked better than gossiping about their neighbours. Combining that with one of those hated developers being in trouble was even more likely to yield information, I hoped.

"I believe significant works have been carried out at the property over the last few months? I have details for an extension to the kitchen."

"They've done a lot more than that. A swimming pool and all sorts. It's been dreadful to live next door to. Vans arriving at all hours, doors slamming, men shouting to each other. Absolutely no consideration. The Residents' Association tried to take it up with them but got nowhere. No-one seems to know who actually owns it. A development company, I think."

"Really? We've been informed that some of the people involved are on our blacklist but operating under other names. I wonder, could I show you some images? We'd very much like to put a stop to their activities before they disturb other council taxpayers."

"Of course. Do come in. The light's better if you need me to look at photographs."

"Thank you so much." I followed her into the hallway and fussed the dog. "What a lovely Lab. Such a friendly breed." She smiled broadly. Even if I disliked them, I'd learned to always praise dogs and children. "I'm afraid the photos aren't very good." I pulled out my phone and opened the folder so that I could swipe through them.

"No, they aren't terribly clear, are they?"

"I know, but sadly I'm not allowed to show you the police mugshots and so these were obtained covertly."

"Mugshots? Nasty pieces of work, then."

"We've no evidence that they're dangerous, but they're probably best avoided." I swiped through the pictures slowly.

"Him. Definitely him." She pointed to the man identified by the bartender at the Pack Horse. "Coming and going at all hours in his massive Range Rover. He owned the place, I think."

"I see. Thank you so much. It's as we thought. And this woman?" I flicked to a picture of Bea.

"Yes. That lovely hair, you can't miss it. She was here quite frequently, usually at the same time as him and often in the evenings. I think she must have been the interior designer or estate agent. I imagine she found him difficult to work with. A couple of times I heard raised voices and then the door would slam and she'd drive off. Too fast, I might add, for an area like this with lots of children and dogs."

"How annoying for you." I tilted my head to one side, appearing sympathetic as I gave silent thanks for nosy neighbours. "Did you hear a name by any chance? I'm not sure what aliases they're using at the moment."

"I'm afraid not, but they were definitely here."

"That's really helpful. Thank you so much for your time." I smiled and bent to pat the dog again.

"I'm happy to help. It's been a nightmare to live next door."

As I walked down the drive, I was smiling broadly. I now

knew for sure which of the men was J and the records relating to this house might even give me his name.

Back in the car, Mum was looking fidgety. It was too dark to read now and I'd been longer than she'd expected. I got in and grinned at her in the light of a streetlamp.

"Anything useful?" She looked doubtful. "You were a while."

"Definitely. I know Bea and her chap were meeting here, often in the evenings, and that he probably owned the house. I know which of the three men in the photos is him and what sort of car he drives. I know the property has been sold recently but people aren't certain who the owner is or was."

"Goodness. How on earth did you find all that out?"

"By talking to the neighbours. One thinks I'm a yummy mummy looking for a house in the right catchment area and I told the other I work in planning enforcement at the council." I started the engine and drove off.

"You lied?" Mum was horrified.

"Of course I did. If I'd told them the truth they wouldn't have been half as forthcoming. And if they know this bloke Bea's been seeing, they might have alerted him that I was on their trail. Nothing I said would arouse suspicion."

"You're quite the detective." Mum seemed surprised. I wasn't sure how she thought I normally got information out of people.

"I have a number of personas I can trot out when I need them, Mum, from VAT inspector to oligarch's girlfriend. You just have to observe your mark and pretend to be the sort of person they'll feel comfortable talking to."

. . .

On our drive back to Worcester, I felt pretty optimistic. An evening's rummaging through online records would hopefully give me the name of the property's owner or the architect who drew up the plans for the planning application and then I should be able to find out all sorts of other information. If none of that led me to Bea then I'd just have to doorstep him at his home or office, depending on what I could turn up.

Given how careful he'd been to keep Beatrice a secret from his wife, the threat of blowing his life apart would encourage him to tell me everything. If he wouldn't or couldn't, then at least I'd have some leverage with which to persuade the police to take Bea's disappearance seriously. I'd go back to Albert Road the following evening, I decided. If no-one was in, I'd find a way into the garden and have a look around.

"You're quiet." We were halfway home, stopping and starting in the rush-hour traffic and Mum still hadn't spoken, although in my peripheral vision I'd caught her looking at me a couple of times. I hoped I wasn't in trouble for fibbing to the neighbours.

"Just thinking."

"About what?"

"About you. I've never really thought about your job before but I've seen you in a new light this afternoon. Tracking people down and finding things out. Making progress."

"Lying through my teeth."

"That too. As a parent, you don't think of your children as being knowledgeable and competent. Even Anna, she's a doctor but I still struggle sometimes to accept that she knows what she's talking about."

"And you don't know enough about my life to see that I'm good at my job?"

"Exactly. But I'm starting to understand that you get things done."

"I try. But with Bea, it feels as though I'm just chasing shadows."

We fell quiet again, but as I looked out at the sea of red lights in front of me, I hoped that today I'd given a form to at least a couple of those shadows and that I was a little closer to finding Beatrice.

17

My conviction that I'd made a significant step forward was soon shattered. I spent the evening ferreting around the internet, searching planning applications, Companies House records, and endless databases and come up with virtually nothing. This was a property developer who appeared to have no website, no history, no tangible existence. All I could find, at the Land Registry and on a pdf of the planning application at the council site was the name of a business: Lark LLC. But tracing Lark only led me to the dead end of a shell company based in the Caribbean. It seemed excessively secretive. Whoever J was, he didn't want to be identified. He and Lark seemed to be as cagey as Bea.

But I'd made progress and although this was a hurdle, I had plenty of ideas and possibilities to pursue. Early next morning, I emailed Ben to ask whether his digital wizardry could find out any more about Lark or point me in the direction of someone who could.

It also crossed my mind, that Bea might have disappeared because she was hiding from someone, from J perhaps. But if that was the case, surely she'd have left some sort of false trail to confuse him? This complete absence of information made me wonder whether her disappearance had been a choice at all or due to something altogether darker.

I decided to head back to Edgbaston that evening, banking on darkness giving me enough cover to get into the grounds of number 27. I wasn't sure what I was hoping to find and one of the things that had kept me awake was the fear of what might be hidden there, my subconscious forcing me to acknowledge that Bea might be dead, even though my waking brain refused to let that idea cross my mind. But those texts from J had gradually become less romantic and more controlling and I knew how those relationships worked. Men like that wore you down and could explode in violence when you finally stood up to them.

When I got home from my morning run, Mum and Dad were up and pottering about. I made a cuppa and sat down to scan my emails, wanting to ensure that I had a business to go back to when I found Bea. I kept saying 'when' I found her, not letting myself consider the implications that came with saying 'if'.

Jason, my tech-billionaire client had emailed from Palo Alto, full of excitement about some Georgia O'Keeffe flower paintings that were coming up at Sotheby's New York in a few months.

He also wanted to check that I'd added his birthday celebrations in Las Vegas to my diary. An outstanding year at his company had prompted him to organise a weekend trip for his senior staff, friends and family. And random people like his art advisor and her partner, it seemed. Vegas had never appealed to me, a bit vulgar perhaps, but if anyone knew how to throw a good party it would be Jason.

And Pierre from Interpol was still trying to contact me. I sighed. He wanted information about a Caravaggio that I was pursuing. I wasn't keen to talk to him just yet as I'd prefer to recover the piece myself, if only for financial reasons.

To them, and more, I sent holding emails, asking them to bear with me. I had no idea when I'd be back at work, but hopefully it would be soon.

DISTRACTED by the prospect of my night-time exploring, and knowing that I wouldn't settle to much that was productive in the meantime, I set off for Charlecote Manor in the Cotswolds. It was another place I'd identified as a possible location for one of J and Bea's trysts and I hoped I might wheedle some information or even a few frames of CCTV out of them.

A few miles outside Tetbury, the Manor was beautiful in spite of the March drizzle, from the mellow stone of its walls, to the red tiles of its roof, the gables, the gardens. Even the gravel was perfect. I rather fancied paying a visit sometime and thought I might suggest it to Pete.

But despite all that perfection, it wasn't a fruitful trip. I couldn't be bothered with adopting a persona and just explained to the manager that I was a worried friend who'd been roped in to find Beatrice and that I knew she'd been here for lunch on the 6th February.

I did hint that we'd probably got sufficient information to go to the police now, and that may have persuaded them to check their bookings for me, aware that telling me what I needed to know might save them from having the boys in blue traipsing through their reception and putting off their very posh guests.

But it was no use. Although the manager found the booking, it was in Beatrice's name and the contact details they had were her office email and mobile phone number. The phone she hadn't been answering for the last few weeks.

So I smiled and thanked them, took a brochure, and set off home. The traffic to Worcester was slow, stop-start all the way, and when I turned into Mum and Dad's drive it was after four. Just time to wolf some food before getting changed into my night-time prowler gear prior to heading back to Edgbaston for a look around the exterior of 27 Albert Road.

YAWNING DESPITE A DAY of too much takeaway coffee, I paid only cursory attention to the unfamiliar car outside Mum and Dad's place—a silver BMW with a hire firm's sticker in the rear window. I went in, planning to say a polite hello to the visitor and then disappear to the dining room to sort out the next day's plan to visit more hotels unless Ben came up with something more useful. All my legwork seemed to be ruling things out, and I was intent on making some progress that ruled a few things in.

A jacket was lying on the hall chair—black, outdoorsy, an unusual logo on the sleeve. I knew someone with one just like it. Then I heard voices and although I could only pick up tone and pitch, not actual words, I realised who the visitor was. I picked up the jacket and sniffed the familiar scent, wanting to be sure, and my heart leapt. I paused at that, and reminding myself to play things cool in front of Mum, I went into the sitting room to greet our unexpected guest.

My mother was at one end of the sofa, a small table

pulled up beside her with a tea tray on it. At the other end, clad in jeans and a blue shirt, twenty-four hours of stubble on his jaw, cup and saucer in hand, was Pete. He grinned when he saw me and stood up. Mum was smiling as she began to pour tea for me and I could tell by her smug smile that her thoughts had jumped ahead to the hat she would wear as Mother of the Bride.

"This is a surprise." Pete and I hugged politely, and I breathed in his familiar warmth, my senses already tingling. "What brings you here? I thought you were in Syria." I was smiling although I knew there was a warning in my eyes. Surprises like last weekend when he came home unexpectedly were lovely but this one was going to come with a side-order of maternal interrogation.

"Our news crew decided to take a few days R&R, and I did the same, especially as I was booked to go on leave next week anyway. You sounded fed up, so I thought I'd offer my services if you can make use of me?" Pete smiled; he loved that I was squirming. I sat down to drink my tea.

"Isn't that thoughtful, Kate?" Yes, Mum was already thinking about churches.

"So thoughtful," I echoed. "And where are you staying?" As well as 'Kate's room' where I slept and random household items gravitated to, there was a proper guest bedroom, all matching bedlinen and carefully arranged cushions. It was selfish, but I hoped Pete had sorted out digs; I didn't fancy a chaste few days in separate rooms, snogging like teenagers when no-one was looking.

"Well, your mother has very kindly invited me to stay here, but I booked a holiday let online while I was hanging around the airport in Dubai. I'm staying in town, near Britannia Square, in a converted stable at the back of one of the big houses."

"As long as you're certain you'll be all right there." Mum looked concerned.

"I'll be fine thanks. I dropped my kit off earlier and it looks very comfortable. As well as helping Kate, I just want to catch up on some sleep."

"You must make sure Kate doesn't work you too hard and lets you get some rest. She can be very demanding."

"Oh, I'm fully aware of that, Mrs Carpenter." Pete winked as Mum glanced round at me, and I shook my head. When I'd pulled into the drive, he was the last person I'd expected to find sharing tea and shortbread with my mother. At least he'd side-stepped her hospitality, presumably also feeling that we were too old for stolen fumblings while we tried not to wake her and Dad up.

"I should probably bring you up to speed." I decided to move the conversation on before Mum started questioning us too closely.

"That sounds good." Pete smiled. "Any luck today?"

"Not so much, but there are a couple of things I'd like your input on. Seeing as you're here and all."

"You two carry on. Don't worry about me." Mum waved us away, adding to Pete, "Kate seems to have adopted our dining room as her office."

"Come on through." I stood up and handed Mum my empty cup, refusing to acknowledge her meaningful looks.

Pete caught my hand as he followed me into the dining room and I turned to him as he shut the door. I kissed him and exhaled slowly, savouring the feeling of having his arms around me again.

"This is ridiculous. You know that, don't you?" I laughed, pulling away a little.

"Completely. But I missed you and you were worried

about Bea so I wanted to help. As I managed to get off early I hoped you'd think it was a win for both of us."

"Thank you. My mother will be unbearable though. She was convinced you were potential boyfriend material just from that phone call the other day. And it's nigh on impossible to keep things from her. She's bound to realise you're not simply some bloke I work with now and again."

"Sometime she'll have to know. Is it such a bad thing if she twigs? Really?"

"Yes. I don't tell her anything about my love life. None of my family are aware of even half of what happened with Chris. And ever since then, all Mum wants is for me to find my Prince Charming. Kolya didn't make the grade but now she'll think you could be him."

"Perhaps I am?" Pete kissed me again, his hands tightening on my waist, keeping me close.

"You're more the big bad wolf. And I like that."

"You're mixing your fairy tales up, darling. So what's the plan? How about you get me up to speed about Beatrice over dinner and then I lure you back to my stable for a night of passion?"

"Maybe later, Casanova. First up, we're off to Birmingham for a spot of trespassing. Possibly a little breaking and entering if the locks don't look up to much."

"Really? It can't wait?" Pete murmured in my ear, his lips making their way along my jawline, his breath stirring the hair on my neck. My pulse quickened.

"No. It's got to be after dark and tomorrow night's not possible as I have to go to Anna's."

"Ah yes, dinner with the family. Your mum's already invited me." He was grinning, enjoying teasing me.

"Don't do this. Or I won't come to your place later."

"Rubbish. You know you can't resist me."

"That's very true." I shook my head. "How about we pick up a takeaway on the way back from Birmingham and then you can show me your stable?"

"It's a very lovely stable with an absolutely massive bed and a shower easily big enough for two."

"Good to know. Now go. Put some dark clothes on that are suitable for climbing walls."

"You're not coming with me?"

"No. I'll pick you up in an hour or so. We have to maintain some sort of facade for my folks. I have to gently find out when my curfew is. I can't just grab an overnight bag and announce I'm off to your place for the night."

"But that is your plan at some point?"

"If that's okay with you?" I raised an eyebrow.

"Have I ever turned you down?" Pete kissed me and stepped away, pulling out his phone. "I'll text you the address and see you in a bit. Hurry."

I DID HURRY, though perhaps not as much as Pete would have liked me to. Once I'd waved Pete off, joined on the doorstep by Mum, I considered the contents of my chest of drawers. I'd packed quickly and without a lot of thought—the four inch Louboutin heels were testament to that—and I didn't really have outfit options that would take me from climbing garden walls to a spot of seduction, so I dressed for the former in leggings, trainers, t-shirt, and a hoodie with a deeply unsexy but effective sports bra underneath. Rummaging about I found the woolly hat and neck warmer I'd brought in case the weather turned colder. I'd need those to hide my face.

Mum came into my room as I was packing the more practical elements needed for the evening's outing—tiny halogen torch, lock picks, cable ties, a discreet (albeit illegal) can of pepper spray, black latex gloves, telescopic baton. The sort of thing every woman takes on a date.

"It's very nice of Pete to come and help you. He seems like a lovely man."

"He is." I side-eyed her, knowing where this was going.

"I think he's very keen on you."

"You reckon?" I grinned, despite myself.

"I saw the way he looked at you. His face lit up when you walked in the room. And he probably needs a rest but he's rearranged things to be here for you."

"I'd do the same for him." I started to twist my hair up into a clip.

"Then maybe you feel the same too, if you'd only admit it to yourself." Mum sounded pleased and I wondered whether I should tell her about Pete and me. But where to start? "What time will you be home? And do you have your key?"

"I don't know when I'll be back and yes, I have my key. I might be late. Very late." I added, testing the water.

"Or maybe you should just admit you'll be home in the morning?" Mum smiled. "Have a nice time and be careful in Birmingham." And she was gone, off to finish making dinner for her and Dad, leaving me rather taken aback. I shook my head; she knew, she bloody knew.

Deciding that I might as well take advantage of this unusual permissiveness, I threw some jeans, an old cashmere jersey, and clean underwear into my bag along with moisturiser and my toothbrush, then legged it, calling a cheery farewell over my shoulder.

. . .

Driving into town, I was struck by a pang of guilt. Beatrice was still missing and I was now properly worried about her. Even though we were off to Edgbaston first, I was looking forward to having dinner with Pete afterwards and spending the night together. But planning to take time out to spend with him felt wrong.

But surely, I reasoned, a bit of a break was okay? And I would be able to cover more ground with him to help me. He'd acquired many skills in the Army, some less useful in civvy street, but tracking people was one I could use. And I was weary of worrying about Bea; I needed a rest from that, if only brief, in order to keep going. The prospect of having someone to lean on rather than carrying it all myself was a huge relief.

I carried on justifying it all the way to Britannia Square, the centrepiece of a neighbourhood of white-painted Georgian houses. I justified it when I turned into the drive and parked next to Pete's car. I justified it when I walked across to his converted stable. But when he opened the door and smiled, that lazy smile that promised so much and always made my heart beat faster, I have to confess that Bea went clean out of my mind for a moment.

18

"This is gorgeous." I looked around the cottage. Simple and luxuriously rustic, all reclaimed parquet flooring and linen-covered sofas, there was little hint of its former life as a stable.

"And so are you." Pete kissed me and I smiled.

"That's very chivalrous darling, but I'm dressed for work. And look at you, Action Man." Like me, he wore all black—outdoorsy trousers, boots, and a close-fitting t-shirt. I ran my hands up his chest and linked my fingers behind his neck as he pulled me closer, glad to have him safely back from the Middle East again. Pete cupped my face as he lowered his head to kiss me and I stepped away. "Nope. Time to get going."

"Really? We have to leave now? Not in an hour or so?" He kissed me again and I shook my head.

"No, now. Because once we've done what we need to, we can come back here and I'm all yours, all night. It seems Mum has realised that I don't spend all my evenings knitting at home by the fire. She said she'd see me in the morning."

"Crikey. We'd better get going. I'm not hanging around

Birmingham any longer than we have to if I'm on a promise." Pete grabbed his jacket and we left.

Driving up to Edgbaston, I summarised my progress so far. Boiled down to its essence, it didn't sound that impressive. All it came down to was that I had photos and hundreds of text messages, that I didn't like the dynamic of the relationship between Beatrice and J, that I'd identified a number of pubs and restaurants they'd visited and got confirmation on which photo was of J. Not much, really. Ben had emailed to say that he was on the trail of Lark LLC but found nothing concrete yet. This house represented my strongest clue at the moment.

I wasn't looking forward to going there. Unlike setting out to recover a painting, there was no buzz of anticipation. The niggling sensation I felt wasn't excitement, but a cold, pit-of-my-stomach awareness that the house where Bea had been a frequent visitor, could hold a secret. Although I'd refused to allow the 'what if Bea's dead?' question to cross my mind, keeping it at bay by activity and sheer force of will, I might find a clue that would lead me to her, but maybe I'd discover something much worse. Not easily scared, I was nonetheless glad I didn't need to go there alone.

We made a pass of 27 Albert Road before parking round the corner. I zipped my equipment into the pockets of my hoodie, handing some to Pete. He raised an eyebrow at the cable ties, clearly wondering who I was expecting to find, but I simply shrugged, remembering a man delivering a Renoir who'd pulled a knife. Impromptu handcuffs had been useful on that occasion. We both put on neck warmers and stuffed black woolly hats in our pockets. I tucked some latex gloves in the waistband of my leggings and gave a pair to Pete, just in case this turned out to be a crime scene. Then we strolled down the street, for all intents and purposes like any other couple out for an evening walk.

"What's your plan?"

"Over the wall and see what the lie of the land is. Looking at the sales particulars, there are some outbuildings we should check and we'll take a look through the windows to see if there's paperwork lying around that might give us a clue as to who's behind Lark. My picks are in my pocket if we need them."

"That's my girl." Pete grinned. "I do like a woman who plans a break-in so matter-of-factly. And who has her own set of lock picks. I'd get very bored if you were the type who worried about her manicure."

"Handy to have you here though, darling." I squeezed his hand, grateful that he'd tried to make me smile despite my misgivings. "You're the professional and I wouldn't want to break a nail unnecessarily."

From the opposite side of the road, we looked left and right, taking our time to cross over as we checked out what we could see of the house above its wall—no lights, hopefully still unoccupied. Crossing, Pete slipped into the cover of the shrubs on the verge while I approached the pedestrian gate, looking for all the world as though I had every right to. I tapped in another couple of numbers hoping one was the manufacturer's default but no luck. Rather than pick the lock in full view of the street, after a quick glance round to check the coast was clear, I too vanished into the shrubbery.

"Okay?" We both pulled on hats and I adjusted my neck

warmer so that it covered my mouth and nose. I didn't want to show my face until I knew what the security was like.

"Well," Pete eyed the three foot wall with the fence of about four or five feet on top. "I don't do this as often as I used to but I'm sure I'll manage."

He pulled up his mask and we nodded to each other. I took a couple of short strides, jumped to grab the top of the fence and hauled myself up, my feet scrabbling to gain a foothold on the wall. I balanced on the top, pausing for a second while I checked that I wasn't about to surprise the inhabitants. But the whole house was dark, the curtains were open and the driveway was empty, so I threw my other leg over and dropped down into the garden.

Pete landed quietly on the grass beside me and we waited for a few seconds, letting our eyes adjust to the darkness and scoping out our situation. A burglar alarm with a winking blue light was an annoyance, although expected. I swore under my breath as I spotted a camera on the corner of the house and pointed it out.

I hadn't been planning to break in unless I saw something that looked seriously significant or a conveniently unlatched window. The camera bothered me more than the alarm; was it a dummy or was someone in a monitoring centre watching for intruders like us?

"What now?" Pete asked in a low voice, his mouth close by my ear. I was glad he was letting me decide how we approached this. Confident we were hidden in the lee of the fence, I pulled down my mask a little and considered my plan.

"If we assume the camera's real and that someone might be keeping an eye on the feed, even if they call the cops, I reckon we've got at least fifteen minutes before they get here. With gloves, masks and so on, they haven't a hope of recognising us on the footage, so if anyone turns up we'll nip away via the other gardens around here. We'll split up and head back to the car separately. How does that sound?"

"Okay." Pete nodded, squinting at the other corners of the house as he checked for more cameras.

"So, we start at the porch, circle the house and look through the windows. See if there's any sign of occupation, any mail or invoices lying around. Don't forget the bins." I snapped on a pair of gloves and he followed suit.

"Okay. Then gardens, outbuildings and the like?"

"Yes."

"Looking for anything in particular?"

"Something that will tell us who owns this place, any tradesmen who've been working here that we can track down. And be aware of what's around us. You never know."

"Come on." Pete patted my shoulder, understanding what I meant by 'you never know'.

We stepped forward gingerly in case blinding security lights flashed on but all remained dark. Starting with the heavy wooden front door, I shone a torch through the letterbox and though there was no mail, glancing back towards the gate, a silver mailbox glinted in the streetlight. Excellent, that probably had a pretty cheap lock and I'd check in there before we left.

Moving round, we looked in the bay windows—a dining room and drawing room at the front. It was furnished with some immaculately coordinated furniture, but there were no personal effects in evidence and I smiled. Clearly it had been styled for selling and was thus unoccupied. No-one would be driving through the electric gates at any minute.

At the side stood an old coach house that looked to have

been converted. No way through the garden that way, so we crept round the other side, looking through more windows as we passed—a library with a lot of shelves and no books, just more artful ornaments, and another sitting room.

Emerging into the back garden, on our right was a glass extension, huge and inky black, and pressing my nose to the glass I saw the open plan kitchen that the neighbour had mentioned. Nice, in an aircraft hangar sort of way. Automatically, I tried the doors but all were locked. Not even a bi-fold door left unsecured by a careless estate agent.

We crossed the terrace and looked up to see another camera watching us. There was another glass-walled building and we peered in at the swimming pool. It joined up with the converted coach house and through the ground floor windows we saw a small but fully-fitted bar and a snooker table. Open tread stairs led to an upper level and a gym had been built in the space between the house and the bar. It was a man-cave on steroids.

"Crikey. It's a bit flash." Pete didn't sound enthusiastic and it wasn't to my taste either. When in Cornwall, he lived in an old sail loft on the waterfront that he'd mostly converted by himself in the year after he left the Army. It was simple but comfortable and I loved it. But round here, the market clearly liked more bling in its interior design.

By now, we'd circled the entire house and learnt nothing that would help me find Bea. I turned to look down the garden, the outline of shed and summerhouse barely visible in the darkness. For a moment I hesitated. There wouldn't be any helpfully addressed envelopes in those; anything we found was likely to be much more sinister. I'd been dreading this part of the search. The plots of crime novels flashed through my mind and I fought back thoughts of what might be waiting there.

"You okay?" Pete whispered.

"Yes. No. I don't want to look in the sheds." My stomach was tight with nerves I never normally felt but then, I'd never had to face the possibility of finding my oldest friend's corpse before.

"It's okay. I'll do it." He squeezed my hand. Alone, I would have looked, despite my fears, because that was the reason for our visit, but I was relieved he offered to do it for me. "You want to wait here?"

"No, I'll come with you."

We approached the shed first. Pete peered through the window, shining his torch around the interior and I looked at the door, secured with a padlock I'd be able to open in a minute with my picks.

"It's clear. No need to go in there."

We walked down the garden to the summer house. Partly hidden by trees and covered in rambling roses, on a sunny afternoon, it was probably a romantic setting. Right now, to my overactive imagination, it looked every bit like something from a horror film. It was unlocked and Pete swung the door open as I waited with bated breath, watching the beam of his torch scan around before he returned.

"Nothing?"

"Completely empty. Only the garage to check then."

Making our way back up the garden, we went back to the garage at the side of the house. Although I didn't know how to bypass the electric roller on the front, there was also a small door round the corner. Forcing it would make too much noise so I took out my lock picks, squatted down and set to work.

A couple of minutes of delicate fiddling and listening in the dead quiet night, and the lock tumbled open. I stood back and Pete opened the door and entered while I held my breath, palms sweating inside my gloves from a mixture of fear and apprehension. I followed him, shining my torch around.

"It looks okay." He sounded as relieved as me.

I looked about us. Space for two cars, and the light of our torches showed the concrete floor was free from anything that could be blood stains. No chainsaw, plastic sheeting, gallon containers of bleach or anything else with sinister possibilities. Just a garage. Good. A wave of relief swept over me and I exhaled at last.

Then I turned round and on the back wall I saw a chest freezer. One plenty big enough to hide a body. There was no light and no hum, but that it was unplugged meant nothing.

"What's in there?" I could hear the tension in my voice.

"I'll check. Stay here."

My heart pounded as Pete approached and lifted the lid. It was the first time I'd really faced the thought that Beatrice could have been killed. I'd known that possibly this house was a crime scene, but that freezer brought it home, the cold sweat of fear prickling my back. Not for myself—I'd learned a long time ago that the living were far scarier than the dead—but fear that my oldest friend might have met with evil and that she was beyond my help.

"It's empty." I breathed again and smiled weakly at Pete, looking at me in the semi-darkness. "You okay? Shall we get going?" He knew better than to be too sympathetic right now.

"No. We still need to check the bins and the mailbox on the gate. Finish what we came for." My voice shook a little. Keep on, keeping on, I reminded myself.

The wheelie bins were empty and the mailbox full of junk. Unlocking it took a moment and I sorted through the contents quickly—nothing addressed to a person or a company but the new residents seemed to have an extensive selection of pizza delivery firms to choose from.

Looking back at the house, I wondered whether in the interests of being thorough we should get inside and search it, but I had no grounds that would even begin to justify that and a conviction for breaking and entering wouldn't be helpful, professionally speaking. And given the cameras, I reckoned we'd been here long enough.

We returned to the part of the fence we'd climbed in over, knowing that the bushes on the other side would shield us from passing traffic and pedestrians, but as I prepared to jump up, a siren wailed in the distance, rapidly getting louder, getting closer. I swore softly and looked at Pete, who pulled me towards the darkest corner of the garden. We hid there, thorns of climbing roses snagging at our clothes, pressed against the fence, and waited.

The patrol car stopped outside and doors opened and then slammed shut. I caught my breath as the gate rattled, praying that the police officers didn't know the passcode. After a few seconds that felt like minutes, I heard voices.

"What's the point in sending us out here if we can't get in?"

"Search me. The camera people said they saw figures on the monitors but couldn't give any sort of a description."

"Probably just bloody foxes."

"Probably." The fence juddered as one of the officers pulled himself up to look over and we shrank back even further into the pitch darkness.

"See anything?"

"No. Nothing. Think we should climb in and take a look?"

"We'd better. Davis will moan if we don't check. You know what he's like."

"Okay. You wait here if you want." A boot scuffed on the fence and I looked at Pete in horror. We'd need to do a lot of fast-talking to get out of this one.

19

Bracing myself to see the police officer drop into the garden a few feet from us, sure that we'd be spotted, the crackle of a radio broke the silence. I heard the other cop, the one not likely to land next to us at any moment, speaking and then he called out.

"Joe, come on. There's a disturbance at the McDonald's on the Hagley Road. We need to go."

Joe jumped back down, the bushes rustled as he pushed his way back through them, car doors slammed, and the police car revved away along the street, the evening quiet settling around us again. I let out a long breath that I hadn't realised I was holding and looked at Pete.

"Let's get going." We scaled the fence as before and as my feet hit the ground I stumbled on a tree root, reached out and scraped the wall with the palm of my hand. It stung as grit embedded itself in the skin and I bit back a yelp of pain. Pete pulled his hat and mask off and I did the same.

"Come on. Time to look as though we're just out for a breath of fresh air." He took my hand and we slipped out from the bushes, walking away with as much nonchalance as we could manage. I leaned into him, relieved this was over and that although we hadn't found any clues, nor had we discovered anything sinister.

Driving back to Worcester, my cold, sickening fear had evaporated, but it wasn't replaced by the adrenaline rush that normally accompanied this type of adventure. Usually, I would be coming home with a multi-million pound painting and maybe the satisfaction of outsmarting the bad guys. Tonight, I was happy just to be reassured that my oldest friend wasn't dead in a Birmingham suburb.

Obviously, I'd have preferred to check the garden carefully but the neighbours might be alarmed if we rocked up there in daylight with a cadaver dog or two. I may not be much closer to working out where she was but at least I felt confident I'd ruled out Albert Road for now.

Tomorrow, we would take the next step, follow up another lead. But for now, I planned to enjoy some time out with Pete. In less than a week he'd travelled from Damascus to the UK twice, now giving up the rest I knew he badly needed in order to help me. I was lucky to have him and he deserved to feel appreciated.

"Are you hungry? Fancy dinner?" I asked.

"That would be good. It's a bit late to go out but there was stuff at the stable when I got there so we could probably rustle something up."

"Anything nice?"

"A hamper with posh bacon, eggs, bread, cheese, milk and so on. There's a bottle of wine chilling if you fancy a glass."

"We could have bacon sandwiches," I suggested.

"I do make the best bacon sandwiches."

"You certainly do." I parked next to his hire car and we got out. At the window of the big Georgian house someone dodged out of sight as they saw me look over. "Your landlord is keeping an eye on you."

"Landlady. She's very friendly."

"Oh yes?" I suspected he was being euphemistic there.

"Husband works away much of the time. She did suggest that if I was at a loose end this evening I might like to pop in for a drink. Maybe she meant just a drink, but I'm not sure. She was doing a lot of hair-flicking and arm-patting as she showed me round the cottage." I smiled; for Pete to have noticed any flirting, it must have been pretty obvious.

"Really? And what did you say?" I didn't tend to waste energy on being jealous and I certainly wasn't going to be piqued by another woman showing interest in Pete. Nor had he ever given me reason to suspect that interest from other women might be reciprocated.

"I said I was planning to surprise my girlfriend. I wasn't anticipating that we'd be spending our evening trespassing."

Pete unlocked the front door and we went inside. I pulled off my hoodie and dropped it on the hall chair, turning towards him and running the tips of my fingers over his forearms and biceps, up to his shoulders. I sank into his kiss, warm and safe, and felt the tension ebb away.

"So," he whispered between kisses, "bed or bacon sandwich?'

"You know, normally I wouldn't be able to resist the former, but my stomach is rumbling." I felt a bit guilty at spoiling the moment but a woman couldn't live on romance alone.

. . .

Half an hour later, I'd showered to get rid of the stale sweat of fear—on my own, although I did concede that as per Pete's earlier observation the shower was easily big enough for two—and I'd picked the grit from the brick wall out of my palms. I put on a jersey and nicked a clean pair of joggers from Pete's drawers while the sizzle of frying bacon drifted up to the mezzanine bedroom.

Smiling to myself as I heard Pete pottering in the kitchen, I checked my phone quickly to see if by some miracle Beatrice had replied to any of the messages I'd sent her.

She hadn't, but there was another email from Chris.

The sender showed up as *You Know Who*—a new name to go with a new email address I hadn't yet blocked—and a photo of Pete and me was attached. It had been taken as we stood on my front doorstep, probably when we got back from our walk on the beach the previous weekend. I was reaching to put my key in the lock, one of Pete's hands was on my back and I'd turned my head to kiss him. Judging by the angle, Chris must have been in the same spot as when he'd taken the picture of me after my run, and he must have been waiting for me. After Pete arrived so unexpectedly, it hadn't crossed my mind to keep watch for Chris lurking somewhere.

But this time there was no implied sentiment about how he still missed me.

"I see you've a new man in tow. Have you told him the whole story? What you didn't dare tell the police? I bet you haven't because if you did he'd know that you're just a cheap slut who got what you deserved. But I daresay he'll realise that sooner or later and clear off if he has any sense."

I sat down on the bed, winded as though he'd punched me again. The whole story.

Memories of that night crowded in, pushing their way past the barriers I'd kept up for over two years. The blow that blurred my vision and cracked my cheekbone, the kick that broke my ribs as I fell to the floor, one hand around my throat as he held me down while his other hand pulled at my clothes and grabbed at my body. The fear and the relief of the darkness as I blacked out, coming round only when he'd left.

Just as I'd learned to do two years earlier, I closed my eyes and took deep breaths, concentrating on the in and out, smooth and regular, until those recollections of terror and pain were back in their box. Steely control was all that had got me through it then. That, and the therapist Flora had found for me when she realised that I wasn't handling it all as well as I claimed.

Then, I went to follow the usual plan, to block the address and file the message in case I needed to produce it again one day. Given that he was stepping things up and I was going to have to talk to the police and my lawyer, I assumed they'd want to see these new emails, the ones where he seemed to be making a leap from angry ex to stalker.

But this time I paused. Because as Chris reminded me, there were details I hadn't told the police and the first, and completely reasonable question was going to be 'what does he mean when he says you didn't tell the police everything?' And then what? Would I be in trouble for withholding information? Could his conviction be overturned?

"KATE, BACON BUTTIES ARE ALMOST DONE." Pete called up from the kitchen and I stood up and looked over the railing.

He was trimming the fat from the rashers as I liked it, plates and bread ready, eggs spitting a little in the pan beside him.

"Just coming." I locked my phone and threw it out of sight in my bag.

Pete assembled our sandwiches—thick sourdough bread, a smear of butter, well-cooked but not crispy bacon, slightly runny fried eggs on top—and I leaned in to kiss him on the cheek, watching him arrange everything with, well, military precision. I poured drinks and found napkins while he carried our food over to the table.

"You know, any man who can make a butty this good is probably a keeper." I took a bite and chewed happily.

"All that time I spent wooing you with charm and wit and hot sex and didn't realise this was the way to your heart." Pete raised his glass of elderflower cordial and I clinked my sauvignon blanc against it.

"Thanks for coming to help with this. Searching for Bea feels a little less daunting with you around."

"I'm not sure what I provide apart from some muscle."

"You'd be surprised. Ideas, new ways of looking at what we've found, courage when it comes to investigating sinister sheds. Don't underestimate yourself." Smiling, I stretched out a hand, my fingers linking with his. "We make a good team."

"We do. Although my professional skills aren't especially relevant for this sort of activity. But, you know, if the need arises for someone to abseil out of a helicopter or whatever then I'm the man for the job."

"You're so terribly butch," I teased him. "Tomorrow, we're off to a couple of hotels that I think Bea and J may have stayed at and so we'll see if we can charm any information out of them. I might call in at Bea's office again and see if they've remembered anything about that woman who pretended to be me. And if none of that works, we'll have to pray that Ben comes up with something on Lark."

"And dinner with your family in the evening?"

"Yes. Mum and Dad go over to Olly and Anna's quite often on a Friday. It's nice, everyone together."

"Do you think they'll like me?" There was a hint of uncertainty in his voice.

"Mum thinks you're marvellous already. If only because she wants to see me settled down and you seem willing to put up with me. And Anna's seen a few of our holiday snaps and she's very keen to get a look at you in the flesh." I laughed, remembering her face as she'd looked at the images of a nearly naked Pete in the Maldives.

"Hopefully she won't wonder what you see in me."

"I'm sure she'll realise." I licked bacon fat from my fingers. Pete reached out a hand to cup my cheek and wiped a blob of ketchup from the corner of my mouth with his thumb. "You know, I was such a fool for not acknowledging before how much I love you."

"But at least we've got our act together now," he said, and we sat for a few moments, just looking at each other, ridiculously soppy. I felt a bit guilty, that we should be focussed on finding Bea, but I pushed that thought away just like Chris's email. We'd been searching earlier, aware that we might find her body. Surely that earned me some R&R with Pete?

A FEW HOURS LATER, as we lay among tangled sheets and Pete slept deeply, I was still awake fretting about Chris's increasingly obsessive fury. And his reminder of what I'd kept quiet about.

He was wrong to think I hadn't told Pete though. For all that we initially maintained our involvement wasn't serious, there had always been a lot more depth to it than we admitted, even to ourselves. Contrary to Chris's assumptions, Pete knew all about that dreadful night. It came out in a tear-stained jumble that first weekend we spent together in Geneva, unintended and raw.

He'd asked me how come I wasn't seeing anyone and I'd said that a relationship had ended a few months earlier. I'd told him that Chris had just been jailed for assaulting me and as the need to talk got the better of me I explained that in the attack, he'd raped me as I passed out. Up to that point, I'd only told my therapist the whole story. Not even Flora, although I rather thought she'd probably guessed.

And Pete had been amazing, sympathetic but not pitying, supportive not dismissive. He wiped my eyes and held me close, understanding that some things were difficult to talk about because he carried his own, albeit very different, ghosts with him. Since then, if I'd needed to talk to him, if a memory made it past my mental defences or I had a flashback, he'd always been steadfast.

But what was I going to do now? If I just ignored this email would Chris get bored and go away? Or should I send it to DS Forster and be prepared to tell her the whole story? For the moment, I'd filed it, hoping that out of sight might also mean out of mind, at least for a bit. It was something to come back to when I got home, when I could take the time to think calmly, when I'd found Beatrice.

20

I awoke to soft kisses on the back of my neck and Pete's arm around me, holding me close against his chest. I stretched, luxuriating, and turned to him.

"Sorry, did I wake you?" he asked, knowing full well that he had.

"Evidently so. I think last week's trip finally caught up with me."

"Darling, it isn't due to jet lag that you're still asleep at ten in the morning." He kissed me and I smiled, warm and happy.

"That's very true." And then, wide-awake: "What do you mean ten in the morning?"

"I don't know how to make that any clearer." He held up his wrist so that I could see the face of his watch. "Does it matter?"

"Of course it matters. It's all very well Mum giving me a pass to stay out but I'm pretty sure she expected me back early enough that I could sneak in and we could all pretend I hadn't spent the night with you. Strolling in, late morning, with a grin from ear to ear, is not being discreet."

"So I can't interest you in staying in bed a bit longer?" Pete was amused.

"No. We need to get moving and get to work."

An hour or so later, after a rather awkward pit stop at my parents' house so that I could smarten myself up while Pete wolfed down some of Mum's warm-from-the-oven scones, we were on our way to visit a couple of hotels whose names I thought I'd deduced from Bea's text messages and the diary entries.

Mum, continuing to surprise me, had only tutted a little about the time I rolled home and quite indulgently at that. Maybe she was accepting that at thirty-four it was feasible, indeed reasonable, that I might have some sort of love life.

Or maybe it was because when I walked through the door, Pete was right behind me, most charming smile in place, and she was determined to see him as a future son-in-law, despite the fact that he had almost certainly had his wicked way with her younger daughter. He may not be as ideal as hospital consultant Olly, but she was of the opinion that my ticking ovarian clock meant that I couldn't afford to be too picky.

Our first stop, Kerrick House, was a once-grand, now rather corporate, 4-star establishment advertising conferences and an antiques fair on banners by the front gates. Its park had largely been sold off for a housing development and even as we approached there was a dreary feeling. This place did not feel like somewhere that Beatrice would gravitate towards.

Inside, I explained that I was looking for a friend who'd

gone missing, stressed that it was probably nothing and only a silly mix-up but that her family were worried; the casual excuses I trotted out frequently. As I was passing, and I believed she'd stayed there fairly recently, I thought I'd pop in just to see if anyone remembered seeing her. I smiled a lot, looked worried—hell, I was worried by now—and the receptionist tried to help. I showed her photographs of Bea and J and she checked the register for the dates I thought Beatrice might have been there. She even offered to check to see if the room was booked under J's name but we still had no idea what that was. I left my card in case she thought of anything, thanked her, and went back to the car where Pete was waiting.

"No joy?"

"Nope." I checked the address of the next place and tapped it into my sat-nav. "I'm not getting anywhere. I've worked out all these places but I'm not finding any solid information. And that company name—Lark LLC—I really thought that might get me somewhere but it hasn't. I feel as though I'm falling further behind all the time. I can't believe that I know so little about Bea's life."

"We'll find her." Pete's hand on my knee should have been reassuring but it didn't make me feel better right then. "We just need to keep being methodical. Let's visit this next hotel and perhaps tonight we can think of some new ideas."

"This evening is dinner with my family." I leaned forward, resting my forehead on the steering wheel. "By the time that's over you'll be running for the hills and I'll never see you again."

"No chance. Come on, let's go."

. . .

Knockhampton Hall was a country house hotel near Kidderminster. A sprawling pile with a marquee on the lawn and a peacock patrolling the gravel outside the front door, while inside it was simple and elegant and expensive. The perfect location for an illicit night of passion. Much more Beatrice than the previous place.

We parked and went in and I smiled at the receptionist. This time, I took Pete and his charming smile with me and tried a different tack. A more creative one.

"Hi. I wonder if you can help. I think a friend of mine, Beatrice Copley, stayed here a month or two ago and she was raving about it. But I'm not completely sure that this is the right hotel and she's out of the country at the moment. Would you mind checking the register to see if she was here please?"

"I can't do that." The receptionist's voice was professionally bland. "You know, data protection and so on. We take our guests' privacy very seriously."

"That's such a shame. I don't want to be at the wrong hotel." I smiled and looked a little coy, leaning against Pete's shoulder. "You see, we're hoping to book somewhere for a very special day and she was so complimentary about this place."

"How lovely." The receptionist's demeanour changed in a flash. "Bear with me for a moment and I'll find our events coordinator. She can talk to you about how we could make your day perfect." And with a distinctly more helpful expression on her face, she disappeared into a back office.

"Really? 'A very special day'?" Pete raised an eyebrow. "I'm not saying no, but you seem to be moving things on at quite a pace all of a sudden."

"I reckon the prospect of cold hard cash might ease

some information out of them." I grinned, less soppy and more practical now.

"Good thinking, Batman."

I wasn't wearing anything that looked like an engagement ring but hoped my Christmas bonus ring would pass if no-one studied it too closely and so I slid it from my right hand to my left. And I wondered if I could pull off the giddy bride-to-be act. Pete linked his fingers with mine and winked when I looked sideways at him.

"Smile darling, we're planning the happiest day of our lives, remember?"

The events coordinator came back and shepherded us towards a couple of sofas, sending the receptionist to fetch coffee. Introducing herself as Julie, she was in her late forties, immaculately groomed and beady of eye.

"So how did you two meet?" She was smiling broadly, notebook still closed in front of her on the low table, a card folder underneath. We would have to improvise here as I didn't think 'when he helped me put on a bulletproof vest' was going to give quite the right impression.

"At work. Couple of years ago." I smiled.

"How lovely—your eyes met across the photocopier."

"Something like that."

"And where do you work?"

"We're both in the art business." It was probably best to keep it as truthful as possible. "My friend stayed here I think, a month or two back. I know it's terribly cheeky, but I'm worried that I've remembered the name of the hotel incorrectly and I'd hate to waste your time if I'm really supposed to be somewhere else. She's away at the moment so I can't check with her." I thought we might move things along a bit as I didn't want to have to work up an entire backstory for our engagement.

"And I'm impatient to start getting the wedding organised. I can't wait to be married to you, Kate." Pete twinkled his eyes at me and I trod on his foot, out of Julie's line of sight, warning him not to overdo it.

"How lovely. Well, you'll be glad to know that it was here that Miss Copley stayed so you are in the right hotel." Julie seemed thrilled by this. Even more so than me. I wondered how big she thought the budget for our nuptials was. Opening the cardboard file, she pulled out a sheet of paper. "Miss Copley stayed in the Laburnum Room, one of our loveliest with a view over the gardens. She and Mr Whittaker were here for just one night. Wednesday 20th January. Actually, I remember them." Julie smiled, amused.

"You do? I haven't met him yet."

"Well, yes. You mustn't tell her I told you this but it was quite funny."

"Funny?"

"Yes. She got here alone and he arrived late in the evening—ten o'clock or so, I think. Miss Copley came down and met him in the hall and they went to go upstairs but he hadn't checked in so I had to call him back. And there was all sorts of bother because he'd left his wallet with his identification and so on at work."

"Goodness." I wondered where 'funny' came into this.

"I know. Anyway, I think your friend was a little annoyed with him for being so late and I didn't want to make matters worse so I just got him to give me his details. It's so rare that we need to check up. It's more in case there's a fire or something so we can account for everyone. And then he left really early. About five am. So I'm afraid your friend's stay here wasn't perhaps as romantic as she had hoped." Julie smiled ruefully and taking her cue I did the same.

"I can imagine. Men just don't get romance, do they?"

"Not like we women do." Julie nodded sympathetically at me, bonding over the general uselessness of our partners.

"We're hopeless, but I try my best, don't I?" Pete squeezed my hand.

"You do, darling. I do hope this chap has sorted himself out now. I can't imagine Beatrice putting up with that for long." I sipped my coffee. "What was his name again? I don't think she's mentioned him recently but we're due a proper catch up soon."

"Whittaker. Jonathan Whittaker." Julie's eyes flicked down the paper she'd taken from the file. I fought back the urge to snatch it and run. "The funny part was that one of the girls behind the desk wasn't very impressed with his attitude when we needed him to sign in. She made a joke afterwards that by arriving so late and trying to go straight up to Miss Copley's room, he was actually a client of some sort, if you know what I mean."

And she laughed, dismissing the idea, but I could see a glint in her eye that still wondered exactly what the connection was between Bea and Whittaker. After all, midweek isn't a usual time for a romantic break, and late arrivals and dawn departures did reek of something illicit.

"Oh goodness no, I can assure you it's nothing like that. I've known Beatrice since we were at school together." I was still smiling, my face starting to ache, and I wanted to see what was on that sheet of paper. I remembered Pete wondering whether Beatrice was on the game when I discovered the phone and the stash of naughty knickers. When we found her I hoped she'd laugh about that. But it was time to wrap this up.

"Ouch!" I leapt back as the coffee cup slipped from my hand, covering me in hot liquid. Not too hot though; I wasn't that daft.

"Goodness, are you all right?" Julie also jumped to her feet, snatching a napkin from the tray and flapping it at me.

"I think so. Some cold water, for my hand?"

"Of course, come with me." And just as planned, Julie swept me away to the cloakroom, leaving Pete on the sofa with the sheet of paper with Jonathan Whittaker's details in front of him. As I glanced back, he gave me a discreet wink and reached for his phone to take a picture.

"SO WHAT HAVE WE GOT?" I turned to Pete when we got back in the car. After fussing over my wrist and hand for a while, Julie and I had returned to where Pete was reading the newspaper. He remembered to feign concern over the possible injuries caused by 50ml of tepid coffee and we'd managed to get away with a thick brochure and a promise to return and look at the facilities for our 'very special day' as soon as we could.

"Here." He pulled up the picture and passed me his phone. "A productive visit I think."

I zoomed in on the image—he'd given his name as Jonathan Whittaker and an address in Leeds.

"Shall we go now?" I looked at the clock on the dash. Half-past two.

"Not if we're going to your sister's this evening."

"But we've got an address." I was torn.

"How about driving up there tomorrow? It's Saturday, we can get there early, when he's most likely to be around. Catch him off guard." Pete was right. Charging up to Yorkshire now wasn't going to help. Arriving first thing the next day, considered and ready for anything was a better idea.

"Okay. This is progress though, Pete." I looked at the

image again. "This is the biggest bit of information I've found. This could lead us to Bea."

21

Given that a trip to Leeds wasn't an option, I decided to take a detour to Bea's office on the way back, thinking I'd see if anyone had come up with any useful thoughts. And I had those photos. Maybe one of those might jog someone's memory. I wasn't optimistic but it wouldn't hurt to remind the staff of MacGregor and Wise that I was still looking for information.

"They might not know much about Whittaker, but you never know," I suggested with a shrug.

"Absolutely. Or they might have remembered a bit more about the woman who claimed to be you."

"True." I gave that some thought and had an idea, something to try. "Stay here. I won't be more than a few minutes."

When I walked into the reception area, I noticed the red, blinking, after-the-horse-has-bolted eye of the CCTV keeping watch. Stacy's professionally bright smile faltered as she saw me.

"Good morning. Do you have any news?"

"Not much really. I'm still following things up." I didn't

want to let on how worried I was or just how little I'd managed to find out so far. "You've not heard anything?"

"Not a word. And we would have called you straightaway if we had."

"Thanks. Fingers crossed I'll run her to ground soon and she'll be horrified that she's caused us so much worry." I smiled encouragingly; there was no point making Stacy feel worse. "I wonder whether you could look at some pictures for me, see if you recognise any of them?"

First, I showed her the three men. She took my phone and swiped back and forth between them, shaking her head slowly.

"Sorry. None of them look familiar."

"It's okay. What about these women?" I pulled up a picture and handed the phone to her. "Were any of them the one who came here and claimed her name was Kate Carpenter?"

I showed her five photos, including two random friends of friends whose images I'd grabbed from Facebook, just to see if she could actually remember what the woman looked like. I had no idea if my hunch was correct, but something that had been niggling at the back of my mind had finally crystallised.

She studied each in turn and then asked me to go back to the third image.

'Her." Stacy passed the phone over. "That's the woman.'

Gotcha, I thought, looking at the photograph. Now I knew where I'd be paying my next visit today.

When we were at school, Joanna Wilson had been what's known as a frenemy nowadays. We hung around in the same group of a dozen or so girls, and she was its self-appointed leader.

I'd never had a lot of patience with that dynamic and besides, I was irrelevant to her. She put up with me solely because I came as a package deal with clever, pretty, petite Beatrice. We were friends in name only. I put up with Joanna and her acolytes because it was less hassle than having them hate me. I never understood what Bea saw in there. Maybe she also felt that it was easier to be on the inside of the group rather than a potential target.

I was too geeky, too tall, read too many books, listened to the wrong music and after the London trip where I ignored Oxford Street in favour of the National Gallery where I could drink in Seurat's Bathers and Stubbs' monumental equine portrait of Whistlejacket, they stopped hiding the fact that I didn't fit in.

But it wasn't as an old friend hoping to catch up that I arrived at Joanna's converted barn in the countryside near Malvern. I'd left that persona behind in the Cannonball a couple of nights ago. Now, as I parked next to her Discovery and strode across the gravel towards the back door, I was firmly in my guise of slightly impatient investigator wanting answers.

I rang the bell and waited, glancing back at Pete leaning against a garden wall in the sunshine looking bemused. Family detritus littered the small conservatory that seemed to act as a porch—kids trainers and wellies, a dog bed, pegs overloaded with coats, an expensive pair of brown suede boots of the type beloved by yummy mummies.

Joanna opened the inner door and stopped dead, looking at me through the glass for a moment and I saw a multitude of emotions flit across her face from irritation to fear, before she settled on pleased to see me with a hint of but-I'm-very-busy-and-only-have-a-minute.

"Hi. What a lovely surprise. Was I expecting you? We're so out of the way here that we don't tend to get people dropping in." It was a very forced smile. Her gaze flickered across to Pete, curious and possibly slightly intimidated by the fact that I seemed to have a minder with me, but she said nothing.

"Let's not waste time. I need to talk to you. Are you alone?"

"Yes. Tim's at work and the au pair's taken the kids to a playdate." Her face fell. She knew why I was here.

"Good." She stepped back and I went in, following her into a huge kitchen with the obligatory Aga belching out a comforting warmth. Automatically, she picked up the kettle then paused, unsure what the social protocol was.

"Tea. Just milk. Not too strong." I dropped my bag on the table and leant against the dresser, waiting in silence while she made two cups of tea—Emma Bridgwater mugs, natch, to go with the Aga—and then Joanna sat down at the scrubbed pine table. I continued to stand; sitting down felt chummy and I wasn't in that sort of mood.

"So," I began, "tell me why you went to Bea's office looking for her and why you told them your name was Kate Carpenter."

"I haven't hurt her or anything, you must know that." Joanna's voice wavered and I saw her hands trembling as she gripped the mug.

"I didn't say you had." To be honest, that hadn't crossed my mind. If she had harmed Bea in any way she wouldn't have turned up at her office two weeks after she disappeared unless it was part of a plot more elaborate than I thought her capable of. And I definitely didn't think she had the guts to kill someone. "Why were you looking for her?"

"I've been a fool." Joanna dropped her head, burying her face in her hands for a few seconds. "To start at the beginning, things between Tim and me haven't been great. He's stressed at work, I'm fed up with living in the middle of nowhere and having to spend my life ferrying the kids around. We've been really snappy with each other for a while."

She paused and I waited, sipping my tea. I kept my expression neutral but I was remembering their university romance, the lavish wedding in a castle, her smugness at bagging the soon-to-be-successful husband from the wealthy family. In fact, I recalled, she'd still been smug about her supposedly perfect life in the Cannonball a couple of nights earlier.

"At a barbecue in the summer, Susie's husband—you've met Will, haven't you? Anyway, they've hit a rocky patch and he's a dreadful flirt at the best of times, but it got out of hand and we ending up snogging like teenagers behind a hedge in their garden." She shook her head and I had the impression that she was finding this cathartic. "We shouldn't have, but we met up for lunch the following week and then we started seeing each other more often. At first, we only talked, about our marriages and so on. I think both of us found it helpful to share our problems. But then one day he took me to look at a house he'd just taken on his books. Did you know he's an estate agent?" I nodded. "The owners had moved out but left a lot of furniture and we were looking around the master bedroom and well, we got carried away."

"And this started last summer?" I was trying to see how it linked up with Bea's relationship with J.

"We first slept together in September. And since then it's

become a regular thing, once or twice a week. Sometimes we have lunch, sometimes we just meet at one of the houses he's selling. It's easy for him to make excuses to be out of the office for a couple of hours or so and I'm on my own all day now that the twins have started school." She looked up at me, a flash of the old teenage entitlement crossing her face. "I'm not proud of it, but we couldn't help ourselves."

"Of course, you could." I wasn't about to waste my time listening to her justifications. "You could have said no. Instead, you felt bored, he was available, and you didn't see anything wrong in helping yourself to your best friend's husband."

"You've probably done things just as bad."

"Nope." I thought about my own romantic history. I'd made some ill-judged choices but none of that nature. "But how does this tie in with Beatrice?"

"Will and I had planned a whole day together and I arranged a play-date for the children after school so that I wouldn't have to rush home. We had lunch at Charlecote Manor, down in the Cotswolds. It's a restaurant with rooms. Do you know it?"

"Yes. I was there yesterday." It felt much longer than just a day.

"Well, it was all very nice until I went to the loo and as I crossed the dining room, I saw Beatrice and she saw me. Obviously, she knows Will so it was awkward. I'm not that close to her these days and I had to make sure she wasn't going to tell Susie. So I caught up with her later in the ladies and asked her to keep it to herself."

"And what did she say?"

"She said that of course she would because neither of us wanted our secrets hung out for everyone to see. And that was when I realised that the boyfriend she'd been hinting at for a few months was married."

"Did you recognise the man she was with?"

"No, but Will did. We headed home as soon as we'd finished eating because Will was paranoid." She rolled her eyes and drank her tea.

"And when was this?"

"About a month ago. Early February. I can check, if it's important."

"Later. Anyway, what happened next?"

'Will was a bit shaken. He said we needed to be more discreet and so we've seen less of each other for the last few weeks. Then Susie decided that they should have a huge party to celebrate their tenth wedding anniversary. God knows why; it's like putting a sticking plaster on a broken leg. She invited Beatrice and a plus one and Will panicked that Bea would let slip at the party that she'd seen us. Or she'd bring this man and he'd say something."

"So you tried to contact Bea?"

"Yes. I just wanted to warn her. I'd phoned loads of times but there was no answer and Will was getting impatient so I went to her house. The people next door hadn't seen her for about a fortnight and so I called at her office to see if I could catch her there. They said the same as the neighbours. You need to understand, Kate, if she says the wrong thing it could ruin my life. Will's too." She looked anguished and I smiled, despite myself. Joanna had always loved a drama, nothing had changed.

"I don't suppose Susie or Tim would be too chuffed either." I drained my tea. "Do you have any idea where Bea is?"

"None at all. I had no idea she was planning to go away."

"And did you recognise this man she was with? Had you seen him before?"

"No. Will knows him slightly. Maybe he works in property too? But I don't know his name and Bea's always been very secretive about him."

"Was he one of these men?" I opened the folder of photos on my phone and laid it in front of Joanna.

"That's him." Without hesitation she pointed to the fair-haired man that the bartender at the Pack Horse and the nosy neighbour of the Edgbaston house had identified. "Do you know anything about him, Kate?"

"Nothing much. Except that I think Will might be right about the property thing. Can I have his number?"

"You won't say anything to Susie, will you?"

"Of course not."

"Thanks."

"Don't thank me." My phone pinged as she forwarded Will's contact details. "I'm not concerned with your tacky affair. I just want to find Beatrice. Is there anything else you can tell me?"

"I don't think so. I'm sorry I gave your name to Bea's office."

"Yeah, well, if you hadn't I wouldn't have known about you spotting her with this man." I slung my bag over my shoulder. "But I need you not to tell anyone I'm looking for her. At the moment, I don't know whether she's on holiday or if we should be worried so keep it all to yourself. I'll ring Will and get this man's details from him."

"You can't." Joanna looked panicked. "It's Susie's birthday. They've gone away for the weekend. She thinks it's going to be romantic and get their marriage back on track. If you call him she might find out and she'll know something's up."

"He can think of an explanation, I'm sure."

"Please. You could ruin both our marriages." She looked desperate. "He'll be at work on Monday. Can't it wait until then? It's Friday now, you probably won't be able to do anything over the weekend."

I thought for a minute. We had the address in Leeds to follow up the next day and might not even need to talk to Will if that was successful.

"Okay. But don't warn him that I'll be in to see him." I didn't know how worried Will was about this but it was probably best not to give him a chance to come up with excuses.

"Fine. I won't." Joanna wiped away a self-pitying tear, smudging the black eyeliner than had been her trademark for almost twenty years. I took a step towards the door and then turned back to her.

"And you know something else you should do? Stop being so bloody smug about your supposedly fabulous life and looking down on those of us who've chosen different lives. I might not have the perfect children and the perfect house in the country, but I'm not shagging my best friend's husband either."

And I left, mentally high-fiving myself, both for speaking my mind and for finding another fragment of information.

22

"It feels like a bit of a let-down just going home now that we actually have a name and address for the mysterious J." The road back to Worcester was busy and the endless stopping and starting gave me time to think.

"You reckon?"

"I've been trying to find that information for days. Now I have but I still don't know if I'm any further on. He could have nothing to do with Bea's disappearance. He might be oblivious to it. And then I'm back to the beginning. Worse in fact, because I'm not sure where to go next if that's the case."

"Alternatively, we could turn up on his doorstep tomorrow and Beatrice will open the door." Pete's optimism made me smile. "And if she doesn't, we'll regroup and make a new plan."

"Keep on, keeping on."

"Pretty much."

I was glad Pete was there. Most of the time, at work at any rate, I knew what I was doing and was confident and decisive. And when I needed him to help me, his abilities, his instincts, his mental and physical strength, gave me the backbone to carry on in situations where I'd otherwise be pretty nervous.

Now, hemmed in by dead ends and leads that seemed to disappear like smoke, Pete's presence made me feel like we could find Bea. Hunting for a painting could be more dangerous and involve far more unpleasant people than any I'd come across while looking for Bea, but the emotional side of worrying where she might be was tough. Give me Russian gangsters any day.

BACK AT PETE'S PLACE, he put the kettle on and I sat down to check out the address we had and to see what I could find out about Jonathan Whittaker.

And that concerned me.

For starters, I couldn't track down a Jonathan Whittaker who looked anything like the man in the photo, or one in Yorkshire who was in the property business, save for a Bradford estate agent who was very definitely not Bea's lover.

And the address in Leeds wasn't what I expected. When I located it on a map, it seemed to be an area of closely-packed streets and when I clicked to get an image of the building, it looked like a run-down Victorian pub in an area of fairly scruffy terraced houses. I knew the city a little and it was mostly full of students living in shared digs. Even if the house numbering was off and the image was mislabelled, it wasn't a neighbourhood where people developing expensive places with swimming pools and home cinemas lived. My heart sank.

"I thought we'd found him, Pete. I really thought we had." I waved a hand at the screen, indicating the shabby back-to-backs and even I could hear the bleakness in my voice.

"We don't know for definite until we go and check it out in the morning. And look at all those houses around it. Someone in one of those might have some info." He rested his hands on my shoulders, warm and comforting.

"Maybe." I looked at the image of the old pub again. "What worries me is that this man is trying so hard to cover his tracks. Excessively so, if he just wants to conceal an affair from his wife. What else is he hiding?"

An hour later, we arrived at Anna and Olly's, a 1920s detached house about a ten-minute drive from Mum and Dad's. I'd got changed and given myself a talking to, putting off fretting about what we may or may not find in Leeds until the next day. This was the first time Pete would meet my family *en masse* and I wanted them to like each other. Maybe I did avoid going back to my home town, but I loved my family.

"You ready for this? Every one of them is keen to size you up, see who I've abandoned my vows of chastity and solitude for, working out what on earth we have in common. Trying to get a handle on exactly what's going on between us." I smiled as Pete parked.

"I still don't completely understand that myself," he said. "I expect they also want to be sure that I treat you properly."

"That's true. You've already got Mum on your side so you're halfway there. Mind you, given my advancing age, she's willing to be positive about anyone who'll put up with me." I kissed him and got out of the car.

"Ready?" He held out a hand.

"Not even slightly, Pete. But let's do it anyway." I took his hand and we walked up the path.

DINNER WAS LOVELY. My family couldn't have been more welcoming to Pete. Olly and I fell into our usual teasing banter; he and Anna have been together since I was seventeen and he's the brother I never had. Alice and Jack were sweet in the spotty pyjamas I'd sent them from Paris a few weeks earlier and Anna had cooked a beautiful meal.

"So, what do you think then?" I asked, taking a glass of wine as I joined her in the kitchen and she stirred the beef bourguignon. I'd left Pete chatting to Olly and I could tell Anna was avid for an explanation as to how my involvement with Pete had moved from 'nothing serious' to 'dinner with the family' in the space of a few days. Just as I thought, that was her first question.

"I could hardly leave him at his place on his own, could I? I had to bring him with me."

"Mum said something about the pair of you going to Birmingham. She said you went out with handcuffs and latex gloves in your bag. What on earth were you doing?" I was under no illusions that I could keep Anna off the subject of Pete but I was glad of the diversion.

"No handcuffs, just cable ties in case I needed to improvise. We went to check out the house that Beatrice seems to have visited with this bloke she was seeing. It's empty so we climbed into the garden and had a look round."

"Thank goodness for that. I thought it was part of some kinky sex thing." She took a glass of wine from me and we clinked. "He's quite hot, as good in the flesh as in your holiday photos."

"I have excellent taste. Well, sometimes."

"So it seems." She looked concerned. "But he's not like Chris? I've got patients who are ex-military and have various problems like PTSD. It can make people prone to anger issues."

"No, he's nothing like Chris. In the two years I've known him I've never felt that he could be violent towards me." I felt a flicker then, reminded of the previous evening's email from Chris and wondered whether to tell Anna and ask for her advice, but thought better of it.

"Good." Anna put an arm around my shoulders and hugged me. "And you look very happy, which in turn makes me happy."

THE ONLY STICKY patch came when Mum asked Pete what regiment he'd been in. He wasn't secretive but he preferred to be discreet and usually side-stepped those conversations to avoid the follow-up questions about what he actually did because he really couldn't say much about that. And then people would ask why he left which is something he didn't want to talk about. Still, this was my family, it was probably best that he got used to my mother's rather direct style.

"I was based in Hereford, 22 SAS. Before that, I was in the Parachute Regiment." He passed me the potatoes, still smiling. Special forces soldiers weren't uncommon round these parts; Hereford was just the other side of the Malvern Hills.

"How interesting. Did you get up to anything exciting?"

"Life was often very exciting. More so than any of us wanted at times. I was counter-terrorism for part of the time, intelligence gathering, other stuff." Pete was trying to sound breezy, but I could tell by the way his shoulders stiffened that he knew where this was going. Mum didn't pick up on that though. I laid a hand on his leg beneath the table.

"And why did you leave?"

"I had a few bad experiences and didn't want to be a liability to the regiment so I decided it was time to move on."

"I can imagine it's a very tough job," Anna stepped in. "And now you spend part of your time keeping my little sister safe. Is that any easier?"

"Mostly." Pete smiled and I felt him relax. "She's infuriating at times, but I'm less likely to get shot working with her."

"Kate's always had a mind of her own." Dad shook his head. "And determined. I can't imagine that she backs down once she's on the trail of one of these pictures."

"Dad, the owners and insurers of those paintings pay me a lot of money not to back down." I smiled. "Besides, everyone has to get their adrenaline rush somewhere. Isn't that why you've done parachute jumps, Anna? And Olly, that's why you work in emergency medicine rather than something more peaceful, isn't it?" I looked at the others, wanting reinforcements as I moved the conversation on.

"I suppose so. I like not knowing what's going to happen when I begin a shift." Olly was eating his dinner with one hand, the other arm around Jack who'd decided to sit on his knee eating French beans from his dad's plate. "I'd rather people didn't get hurt, obviously, but when there's a crisis and I can make a difference, that gives me a rush."

"I've never felt a need for adrenaline." Mum looked genuinely puzzled. "I don't know how I've ended up with a family of such thrill-seekers."

"There must be something, Mum."

"Marmalade." Anna said, deftly steering the conversation onwards. "You won first prize at the WI for your marmalade and you were positively triumphant when you rang to tell me."

"Well, I beat Margery Westcott and she's always infuriatingly smug about her so-called secret recipe."

I glanced at Pete and saw him laughing with everyone else, tricky moment over. I felt a little rush of pleasure at seeing him with these people I loved, and a glow of pride at how my family were more than willing to open their arms and welcome him in.

"SORRY ABOUT THAT. I should have warned Mum." I took a dish from Pete and started to dry it. After the table was cleared, we'd claimed the washing up.

"It's fine. It's not unreasonable to ask your daughter's boyfriend about his job. Normally I can head people off fairly easily, but it's only natural for your mother to want a bit more information."

"People aren't as curious if you just stick to mentioning the Paras?"

"Exactly. People know what they do and aren't as curious. The regiment is secretive and so non-military folk are intrigued. And they think it's all some sort of heroic adventure. They don't realise how grim a lot of it is." He rinsed a pan and passed it to me.

"You enjoyed it sometimes, though?"

"Absolutely. And those men are like family. A dysfunctional one, but family. And I've had some amazing adventures and taken part in operations that helped make the world a safer place, but I've also had to see and do things that keep me awake at night. I'm glad I did it, but I'm also glad I left. But you know I prefer not to talk about it. I'm not one of those egomaniacs who wants to strut about making sure everyone knows how tough I am."

"I'm very glad you left. Otherwise I'd never have met you." I leant in across the sink and kissed him. "And I think you're pretty heroic."

"You're biased." He was smiling again now. "But go on, kiss me again."

Apart from that moment when Mum pushed a bit too hard, the evening went well. I managed to avoid thinking about Beatrice and our planned trip for the next morning which was a relief. I needed a mental break from worrying.

Alice and Jack persuaded Pete that they would go to sleep only if he read them a story and while he did that everyone took the opportunity to tell me how much they liked him. Pete was relaxed around them too, talking about rugby with Olly, chatting with Dad about classic cars and the Austin Healey that he'd been tinkering with since Anna and I were teenagers, and about the Antarctic with Mum who'd recently decided to drag Dad there on a cruise as she'd developed a passion to see penguins in the wild.

"Pete's very nice." Anna cornered me again in the kitchen as I was topping up my wine.

"I think so too." I emptied the bottle into her glass.

"Mum will be choosing hats and so on."

"I'm relying on you to manage her expectations. We have no plans to get married and I won't be giving her any more grandchildren. If she wants a third one, she needs to look to you and Olly."

"One day maybe. They are adorable sometimes."

"They're always adorable. Well, apart from the Ribena stain on my white rug and the dent in my Eduardo Paolozzi maquette." Much as I loved them, their visits were quite wearing for me in my very pale, very grown-up flat.

"It's a tiny dent. You'd think bronze would be more robust."

We got back to Pete's place about eleven. There was a holdall dangling from the door handle.

"What's that?" I asked.

"Tommo drove over from Hereford to drop off some kit that might be useful tomorrow, that's all." Pete took the bag, glanced inside and put it in the boot of his car. He and Tommo had met on their first day of basic training and were as close as brothers, still working together now they were no longer in the military.

Inside, I shed my coat and went through to the kitchen to get a glass of water. I'd had three glasses of wine and was feeling expansive. Pete was stone-cold sober and amused.

"My family loves you," I told him. "They've all taken me aside to tell me so. Except Dad, but I can tell he likes you even if he doesn't actually say it. Even Mum approves. She wanted to check with me that she hadn't gone too far asking you about the Army. She's absolutely dogged when she's after information so that's unusually sensitive of her."

"And what did you say?" Pete leant back against the kitchen counter, his hands on my waist.

"Just that you didn't like to talk about it and weren't actually supposed to, but we'd be okay as long as we stuck to your non-operational activities."

"Hence the penguins."

"Indeed. You also had some interesting things to say about elephant seals as I recall."

"They're fascinating creatures."

"Evidently so." I looked up at him, one hand on the back of his neck pulling him close so that I could kiss him. "I love you."

"And I love you too. So very much." We smiled at each other.

"I'm glad to hear that. Perhaps you should take me up to bed and show me?"

"My pleasure." And he swung me up in his arms, kissing me through my laughter as he headed for the stairs.

23

While it felt good to have taken a break from worrying about Beatrice and to have concentrated my attention on my family and Pete for a while, I still woke before six the next morning, ready to get cracking. I showered, dressed, and made coffee and toast, plonking a mug and a plate on the bedside table and bending down to kiss Pete.

"Wakey-wakey Sleeping Beauty."

"Mmm?" He reached out, caught me round the middle and pulled me back towards him. I wriggled and rolled free of his grasp.

"You heard. We're off to Leeds. How soon can you be ready to leave?"

"Ten minutes. Twenty if you allow me time to take a shower and drink my coffee. Bit longer if I can persuade you to come back to bed." He stretched and smiled, optimistic.

"No chance. I'm way ahead of you. We're leaving in fifteen."

"You're a cruel woman, Carpenter."

"Too bloody right. Now get moving." I called back over my shoulder as I went downstairs.

THE MOTORWAYS UP to Leeds were quiet and Pete drove fast. I stared out of the window, not chatting but thinking about what might be awaiting us and what, if any, new information we'd return home with.

When I'd first seen that address, for a fleeting moment I'd anticipated a house like the one in Edgbaston, with Beatrice and the elusive Jonathan Whittaker shacked up in domestic bliss. I would tell Bea how worried people were, she'd apologise profusely and call her mother. She'd introduce us to Jonathan who would be exactly what I'd hope for in a partner for her. A cheating bastard who'd been unfaithful to his wife, obviously, but my vision of how things were going to be sorted out by lunchtime wasn't taking that into account.

After that, Pete and I could have a lovely couple of days together and maybe he'd even manage to lure me into that enormous shower with him at last. Then we could head off to Cornwall to his cottage.

That scenario had evaporated when I'd looked up the address and saw that it didn't gel with my imagination or what we already knew about Whittaker. There was no way that anyone currently lived there and the terraces around it weren't likely candidates either. It was unlikely, but I was hoping that the images online were mislabelled or there was some other mix-up that would be easily rectified once we had boots on the ground.

The drive to Leeds took less than three hours, up the spine of the country. Pete was from Sheffield, about thirty miles or so from Leeds and this trip was the closest I'd ever known him go. I'd tried talking to him about his family in the past, but he didn't give much away. He'd told me that his father did a runner when he was little more than a baby and that his mother remarried and later died of cancer. I knew that he and his stepfather didn't get on, to put it mildly.

Although he'd gone to a grammar school and been expected to go to university, he'd had a few minor run-ins with the police and then joined the Army at seventeen. I was aware that he wasn't in touch with the rest of his family, other than his cousin who was married to my sometime-employer Joe Cathcart. I didn't suggest a detour as we drove past on the M1 so that he could show me the sights of his childhood.

Threading our way through the roads adjacent to the university, the area gradually became less salubrious as we drew nearer to our destination. Large Victorian villas were divided up into bedsits, then came the terraced houses where whole streets were let to students and where the metal security gates on doors and even windows indicated that the crime rate hadn't fallen much in the decade or so since I had friends who'd studied here.

Many of the larger buildings such as redundant churches had been converted into yet more student accommodation and the pubs all proclaimed cheap deals on vodka and Red Bull. Convenience stores, off licences and takeaways were everywhere; Friday night's wrappings littered Saturday morning's pavements and a paper bag pirouetted down the pavement as the wind caught it.

Finding our street, we drove along slowly, watching as housing gave way to a few light industrial units occupied by a second-hand furniture warehouse, a minicab firm and a pizza delivery outfit. We got out of the car and looked at our destination.

The address that Whittaker had given to the hotel was a two-storey building, boarded up and graffitied. A pub once, although I suspected there had been several other incarnations in the interim. A couple of the windows on the ground floor at the front had been knocked out, their curved stone lintels still visible above, so that a metal roller-shuttered door could be installed. Tatty signs unconvincingly claiming the presence of security staff were attached to the railings and to the padlocked gate at the side that led to a row of outbuildings, even more ramshackle than the main structure. There was some blackening around the top floor's windows from fires and heaps of rubbish had been dumped over the railings.

"Not quite Albert Road, is it?" Pete stood with hands in pockets looking at the wreck before us. He didn't look enthusiastic.

"What do you reckon? See if there's a spot that's less overlooked and then in over the wall or shall I try getting that padlock open? It doesn't look up to much." I sounded more positive than I felt.

"You want to go in?"

"Of course. We've driven 150 miles. If we go home now, what have we learnt for all that driving? Nothing that we didn't know from a laptop screen. Besides, Bea wasn't in Edgbaston. What if she's here?" Again, the cold shiver as I had to face up to the idea that something bad might have happened to her.

"Okay." Pete looked at it again, assessing the ways to access it, risks and possibilities. "Fuck knows what's in there. Nothing but rats and junkies probably."

"We have to check." I was matter-of-fact. "I might not if I was here on my own but as you're with me it seems daft not to."

"Fair enough. You got any kit with you?"

"Gloves, lock picks, torch, cable ties, pepper spray, telescopic baton. Usual stuff a girl has in her handbag."

"Come on. We'd better park somewhere less conspicuous and work out a plan."

WE FOUND a posher neighbourhood where the BMW Pete had hired didn't stand out as much and pulled up maps and satellite shots of the building on our phones, looking for a more discreet way to access the site without going over the gates in full view of the neighbours. It didn't look hopeful.

"I reckon the padlock is our best bet. If we try to look like we're just being nosy and chatting and you cover me a bit, it shouldn't take me long. It isn't a fancy one. Just a deterrent really." I was trying to sound purposeful, to push away the same fear I'd felt in the garden in Edgbaston.

"And if not?"

"Then over the gate quickly and hope no-one sees us. At least it's too early for the students to be up and about yet."

Pete opened the boot and we started to fill our pockets with gear. Unzipping the holdall Tommo had dropped off, he handed me a Kevlar vest.

"You think we need these?" I asked, taking off a couple of layers so that I could put it on over my t-shirt.

"I don't know who or what's in there. If there is someone there's a fair chance they might have a knife at least. I'm not risking either of us more than I have to."

"But this is all Tommo left us?" I asked, pulling the Velcro tight and wriggling a bit to get comfortable.

"I'm afraid so. But I'm here and I'm reasonably useful, you know." He grinned, flexing one of his not-unimpressive biceps at me. "I don't think it's the headquarters of a particularly organised gang of hardened criminals."

"That's true." I chucked his fleece across and reached for my hoodie. "Put that on over the top though. We look like cops in these vests."

TWENTY MINUTES LATER, having moved the car to a more convenient location with easy access onto the main roads in case we wanted to leave quickly, we were walking down the road towards the old pub. We were already wearing gloves, and I had a slim lock pick in my hand. The street was deserted. At ten o'clock, it was too early for the minicabs and pizza deliveries, and the student residents were probably still in bed.

As I'd thought, the padlock was heavy but cheap and it only took a few seconds for me to slide the slim metal tool in, sweep it across to flick the locking plate up and pop the hasp open. I put the pick in my pocket, tucked the padlock behind one of the gate pillars and grinned at Pete.

"Easy peasy."

"Okay then, let's see what we've got."

Pete led the way, eyes scanning and every nerve alert as we skirted the buildings, the red bricks crumbling a little where gutters had been leaking for years. I flicked out my baton to poke through some of the rubbish that had been dumped and seeing a couple of syringes lying around I tapped his arm and nodded to them in warning. We both put another pair of gloves on; they wouldn't be much use against a needle stick injury but it was better than nothing.

As I looked at the yard between the buildings, I felt apprehensive. But I pushed that feeling down, tried to focus, to act like a pro, not a terrified best friend. And I realised again how glad I was that Pete was there. Sometimes, it was his physicality that kept me safe; that day it was his mental strength that helped me to control the fear of what we might find.

Towards the back of the site, there was a gap where some of the railings had been pulled apart, enough for a pretty skinny person to squeeze through from the garden next door. Not that it was much of a garden; a patch of weedy gravel where a couple of small hatchbacks were parked beside several crates of beer bottles waiting hopefully to be recycled.

There was still no sign of life and so we moved towards the outbuildings. Pete opened one of the double doors slowly, watching for movement within. Seeing nothing, he swung the big corrugated iron door wider, shining his torch into the dark corners and I joined him on the threshold to peer in.

Damp books with broken spines shedding pages spilled across the brick floor, some slates had fallen in from the roof, a rotten tea chest lay on its side. There were no indications that anyone had been in for a while and nothing indicating a body might be hidden there. I breathed again and Pete laid a hand on my shoulder, understanding my fear.

"Come on then. Let's go inside. We'll start on the ground floor and work up." The door of the pub was closed but the lock was long since defunct and the frame, any vestiges of paint flaked away decades ago, was rotten. Pete glanced at me, checking I was ready, and turned the handle, forcing apart the swollen wood with a nudge from his shoulder.

The building had been gutted over the years and was now one big space with the upper level mostly supported by a few props. A few remnants of pipework clung to the outside walls, the electricity meter was hanging off and it was a long time since it had supplied any power. On the concrete floor, behind the metal shutters, were a few patches of oil where the building seemed to have been used as some sort of garage. The stairs to the first floor had long gone, a few charred timbers showing where they had stood and there was no ladder to give access to the upper level. I was quite glad that we couldn't search up there; this whole structure felt decidedly unsafe and I guessed its next visitor would probably be a wrecking ball.

There were yet more piles of damp and rotting detritus scattered about ranging from floorboards and plaster to plastic beer crates and a slumping stack of damp copies of the Yorkshire Post. Grotty but not worrying. Something smelt bad, a sweetness that caught at the back of my throat. I guessed some of the rats we'd expected had met their ends nearby.

In the far corner was a pile of what initially looked like more rubbish and old clothes on some tatty mattresses. We walked over slowly and I took the baton from my back pocket again ready to flick it open if I needed it. When I heard a cough I realised we'd probably found the junkies that Pete had predicted.

There was no movement and I leaned over to take a look before shaking my head at Pete. The two men who lay there, huddled in filthy sleeping bags, looked to be in their thirties but might have been younger. They were well out of it and I doubted they would be any help to us, even if we managed to stir them. I checked both were breathing, and seeing the blackened spoons and syringes, I felt a wave of sympathy, aware that it was only down to chance and good luck that more of us didn't end up the same way. Despite that, I was also irritated that I couldn't question them.

"How about a coffee down the street? Our friends might

have surfaced in an hour or so?" I nodded in the direction of the two junkies.

"Okay." Pete looked around, checking for anything we might have missed, and started towards one of the corners, nodding at me to follow. The whole place smelt bad but over there it was more obvious.

All pubs had cellars to keep the beer barrels in and the wooden hatch set into the floorboards was the way down to this one. Pete kicked aside some rubbish and bent to heave open one of the doors, letting it fall back with a crash. The stench was even stronger now, dead rat mixed with floodwater, and I heard something scurry and splash. I flicked on my torch and shone it down the hole, the light reflecting off the water.

Pete raised an eyebrow, questioning. I knew that if I genuinely believed Bea might be down there he'd go, but I shook my head. I was sure that she'd never been in this old pub, although I was willing to accept that my conviction may have been at least partly due to my growing desire to get out of the place.

I flashed the torch beam around again, just in case there was a clue down in the cellar, and froze as an arm drifted into sight, fingers reaching out across the water.

24

Shocked, I jumped back from the edge of the hatch, fumbling and losing my torch into the floodwater as I swallowed back the instant rush of bile. Pete dropped to his knees, craning his neck and shining the light of his torch down.

"I can't see clearly. I'll go down." As he got to his feet, I grabbed his arm.

"No. Don't." I'd already seen that the body was face down in the water. "Whoever that is, you can't help them now." I shuddered, nausea rising again. Pete put an arm around my shoulders and gently steered me away from the void as I quivered with terror, wondering if my search for Beatrice was over.

"Stay here. I'll be right back."

Standing outside, I took deep breaths, willing my pulse to slow down and the waves of sickness to ebb away while Pete returned into the building to close the hatch, not wanting the junkies to come round and fall down there. He came back, dusting his hands off on his jeans.

"It's not Bea."

"What? How—"

"I had another look. I can't see a lot but that person's taller and the hair's shorter and a different colour. It's impossible to be completely certain without going down there but I'm pretty sure that body isn't Beatrice." He squeezed my hand. "Are you sure you don't want me to check properly?"

"No. You'll catch something. It's horrible down there."

"I've seen worse." He gave a small, grim smile and I realised again the unknowable horrors of the memories he carried with him.

"Seriously, no." I looked down at my shaking hands. "We should call the police."

"I think so. We can't just leave. You can guarantee someone will have seen us and besides—" Pete shrugged.

"Whoever that is, someone's looking for them, just like we're looking for Bea. I'd like to get them home." I pulled off my hoodie and started to rip open the Velcro of my vest. "You should go and put all this back in the car and I'll call the police. They're going to have a lot of questions and it will be easier to make this sound innocuous if I'm not carrying pepper spray and lock picks."

"It is pretty innocuous, really. We got the address from the hotel and drove up to see if Bea was here. We found it was derelict and took a look round simply because we'd driven all this way."

"Exactly. All we were doing." I tried to be brisk and positive, not wanting to let my mind wander towards what might have been, what might still be. "Nonetheless, we should probably lose the offensive weapons before we start talking to the cops."

"Okay." Pete leaned in and dropped a kiss on my forehead. "I'll be as fast as I can. Promise me you won't go back in there."

"I promise. I'm just going to ring 999 and wait out here for the police." I forced a small smile, trying to reassure him, and took my phone out. I took some deep breaths as he walked away, waiting for the tremor in my hands to steady and dialled the number.

"Hi. Police, please. I've found a dead body."

IT WAS, predictably, hours before we were allowed to set off back to Worcester. A kindly pathologist came to find me as I waited in a police car, sipping takeaway coffee and wishing it was a stiff gin and tonic, and she assured me that the body was definitely not that of Beatrice. That made me feel better, but knowing that a family would have the cops on their doorstep to tell them the tragic news that their loved one had been found in such sordid surroundings, was heartbreaking.

After that, working on the basis that there's always a reasonable chance that the person who finds a corpse was the murderer, West Yorkshire's finest weren't keen to let us go until they'd taken us to a police station to make full statements, to take our fingerprints and DNA to exclude us from their forensics, and told us they'd be in touch. I couldn't see how they would find any useful evidence given the state of the building but they certainly seemed to be making every effort with the arrival of a squad of paper-suited technicians who began searching the buildings.

I managed not to show how shaken I was, battling to explain coherently what had happened. I hoped that they might display some interest in the fact that Bea's lover had given this false address and that she'd been missing for a few weeks, but—understandably really—it seemed their concern was only for the dead man. By the time they let us go I was well aware that we were still on our own in our hunt for Beatrice.

WE DROVE BACK in near silence, Pete leaving me alone with my thoughts, for which I was grateful. Seeing the body in the torchlight, a hand reaching out into oblivion, had finally brought it home to me that Bea might be dead too.

It had been there at the edges of my mind for a while. In the garden of 27 Albert Road, I'd tried to avoid thinking about shallow graves and so on. And when I visited all those pubs and hotels, searched Bea's house, talked to her ill-informed colleagues, every time I checked my mobile to see if she'd replied to my messages or had switched her phone on and would finally answer one of my calls, I'd refused to contemplate that I might be chasing a ghost. But maybe I was.

"So why do you think Whittaker gave that address to the hotel?" Pete asked, somewhere outside Nottingham.

"I called Ben while we were at the police station and you were giving your statement. He says it's owned by Lark. They've been applying for planning consent for years but never got anything through because it was a listed building. Finally, after the fire, it was declared structurally unsound and they gained permission to bulldoze it and put up some student flats."

"Joanna said that Whittaker was in the property business so he must have something to do with Lark. When he had to think of an address fast for the hotel, that old pub obviously sprang to mind." Pete suggested.

"Must have. People don't come up with a fake name or

address that has absolutely no relationship to anything in their lives. Not on the spur of the moment, at any rate, unless they're a spy or something. They use their mother's maiden name, the street they lived on as a child, that sort of thing. Or possibly a derelict property owned by their company." I shrugged and we fell quiet again.

OUR ORIGINAL PLAN had been to go out for dinner at the restaurant where Susie had seen Bea with a mystery man, but neither of us were in the mood by the time we got back to Worcester.

I knew Pete had spotted the way I bit my lip at times when emotions hit me and that he'd noticed how my fingers fretted at the cuff of my jacket. While he drove, every so often, he reached over to squeeze my hand, knowing that the brisk, professional attitude I'd summoned up with the police was a front to hide my fear.

Back at the stable, I took a long shower, scrubbing and scrubbing at my skin to rid myself of the smell of the pub that I was sure was clinging to me, a reek of damp and dirt and death. Once my clothes and Pete's were in the washing machine, the two of us sat down at the kitchen table with mugs of tea and looked at each other.

"At least we ruled out that address. Whittaker clearly lives somewhere else. Possibly not even in Leeds," he said.

"Could be anywhere. Even abroad, if Bea's managed to get hold of another passport. Maybe they're travelling under false identities."

"Not the most likely option, I don't think." Pete pushed a packet of biscuits towards me.

"Nor me, really. In the absence of any known facts, we have to accept it as a possibility though. If I could get into her bank accounts I could see if she's using her cards, and where, but she has all that online by the look of it. The police could check, but the cops I spoke to today don't think there's much chance they'd get involved. Not unless the body turns out to be Whittaker, that is."

"They thought it was most likely to be another addict who'd been squatting there." Pete said.

"I know. To make them take action I need evidence that something bad has happened to her or that we have serious grounds to be worried. My instinct that he's a threat based on all this secrecy and the way I'm interpreting the controlling nature of his texts isn't enough. It's annoying though; they have an arsenal of tools that I don't." I shook my head, frustrated at my lack of progress.

"So we just keep on looking. Although we found the body today and it was tragic, that doesn't mean Bea is any less safe than she was before we came across him. It's unrelated. You need to remember that and stay positive." Pete laid a hand, warm and reassuring, over mine.

"We can't do any more until Monday. Then we'll go to Will's office. I want to talk to him about the bloke who was with Bea when he went to Charlecote for his afternoon delight with Joanna. Hopefully, he'll confirm his name was Jonathan Whittaker and be able to dig up some contact info. If that's a dead-end, I'm not sure where to go next."

"We'll think of something." Pete sounded certain and I smiled, glad that he was there to keep me going.

"We will. And there's nothing we can do right now so we should relax." My feelings didn't match my words. I couldn't imagine switching off until I'd made some progress.

"Does that mean we're taking a day off tomorrow?"

"Looks like it. Unless Ben gets back to me with some info."

"Good. Let's go out and get some fresh air. I think you could do with it." Pete said and I nodded.

"Sounds perfect."

"I know just the place. Have you got walking gear with you?"

"No, but I can borrow some boots. You're not suggesting a gentle stroll and a pub lunch?"

"Not so much. But you'll enjoy it. I promise."

25

I rolled my eyes when I got to Anna's place early the next morning and saw Mum's car already parked on the drive. Anna must have told her I'd be popping in to collect hiking boots and a waterproof. Pete's plan was to drop me off and then go to fill up with petrol and pick up supplies for our walk, insisting that a picnic would be more fun than a pub lunch by a roaring fire. I'd raised an eyebrow at that, unconvinced.

"Your mum's bound to have lots of questions so I won't hurry. Maybe I'll get a coffee and let you have some time together." He was grinning and I gave him a stern look.

"Don't you dare hang around. Back here as soon as you can."

PETE WAS RIGHT. Once I'd hugged the kids, Mum beckoned me through to the kitchen and pinned me down with tea and warm croissants, before making it plain that she wanted to know exactly the nature of my involvement with Pete. My earlier dismissals had been set aside after the family dinner when it became apparent to everyone that we were much more of a couple than I'd let on. And that had got her thinking.

"I'm sure he's nothing like Chris, Kate, but look at his time in the Army, the things he's done." Mum put her mug down and looked at me across the kitchen table. "I mean, it isn't as though he spent his days trotting around at the Trooping Of The Colour, is it? He's killed people."

"That's the case for a lot of people in the military, Mum." But I knew what she meant. There are soldiers and there are special forces soldiers; they're very much a breed apart. It had given me pause for thought when we'd first met. Pete was exactly what I needed in a minder to accompany me on the trail of a stolen painting, but a boyfriend? I hadn't been so sure of that. "He's seen and done things he wishes he hadn't but we're all safer because of people like him."

"I suppose so." Mum didn't sound convinced and I could see why.

"Pete's nothing like Chris. He's not controlling or possessive, he doesn't fly off the handle if I speak to another man. Chris would have been furious about those photos of me with Kolya. Pete wasn't at all bothered because he trusts me. And I wouldn't put myself at risk again. Pete's great. Believe me." I squeezed her hand, understanding her worries and trying to not to let my mind wander towards the question of what might have happened to Bea at the hands of a jealous lover.

"As long as you're sure. Pete does seem nice. And he seems very keen on you."

"So he should be, I'm a catch." I stood up and bent to kiss her cheek, keen to escape before she asked about our trip to Leeds. "And today we're going for a walk in the country."

. . .

The Brecon Beacons stretched as far as I could see to the west, the mountains speckled by a few sheep and groups of walkers, a little early morning mist still trapped in the valleys. On the top of Pen y Fan, I looked at the hills around us and breathed in the air, so cold and crisp and clean. We'd walked up without talking much, save pausing to admire a view or point out a landmark, each with our own thoughts.

I wasn't what you'd call a keen hill-walker, but Pete was completely at home in the mountains, whether relatively modest ones like this or bigger, less hospitable peaks. He said he liked the challenge, the peace, and the clarity it gave him. I was happy to keep him company but it was never going to be my first suggestion for a Sunday morning.

At the foot of the mountain, 800-odd metres below, my mind had been churning with the dead ends and questions that surrounded Bea's disappearance. I kept the memories of yesterday's corpse and the squalor of the old pub away by force of will, focusing on my plan for the next day and the possibilities that might yet lead us to Bea. Pete's quietness seemed more of a philosophical appreciation of these hills.

My whirling thoughts had eased as we'd climbed, and I sat on a rock in the sunshine on the summit, for the moment calm and free of the questions I was trying, and failing, to answer. I could see Pete's point about peace.

I took more deep breaths, feeling the cold tingle in my lungs, and Pete joined me on my rock. He passed me some chocolate and opened a bottle of water.

"What do you think?"

"It's beautiful. I can see why you love it up here."

"Quiet today, and it's still early. In the summer it gets busy."

"I'm not surprised." I looked sideways at him. "What are you thinking about?"

"Everything and nothing. I've been up here dozens of times. In the rain, in the sunshine. For an afternoon's fresh air with a group of mates, training exercises, on my own when I needed to process things I'd seen or done. When I was still in the regiment, this—" he waved a hand at the hills and valleys that surrounded us, "this was our playground."

"A special place."

"Yes. But I've never been up here as happy as I am today." He put an arm around my shoulders. "Now it's special in another way." We kissed and I let my head fall sideways onto his shoulder.

"You're getting soft."

"Perhaps. But if being happy makes me soft that's okay." Then, after a couple of minutes he asked, "What about you? Feeling more peaceful too?"

"Much more. I'm glad you brought me here, I needed a break."

"We'll find her, you know."

"I hope so." I watched the approach of a knot of walkers, all brightly coloured jackets and hiking poles. "Bea took her walking gear with her. I wonder if she came somewhere like this to think as well."

Looking out along the ridges and valleys, the unforgiving nature of the landscape was clear. Bea could have simply got lost and her body was yet to be discovered. I shivered. Or maybe she'd purposely gone up into the hills, driven by some desperation or depression that no-one knew of, and had found a final peace.

Bea had always loved mountains and hiking. That was something she'd shared with Liam, her Kiwi boyfriend. The man she'd so unexpectedly broken up with. The breakup that seemed to have caused such a drastic change in her personality.

"Come on." I stood up, a realisation hitting me. "We need to get back. I have an idea what Bea might have done, even if I don't know why or where she is." And I shoved the water bottle into Pete's hands, heading for the path down the mountain. Loose stones slid beneath my boots as I hurried, scattering walkers making their way up.

"Kate, wait. You're going to injure yourself." Pete grabbed my arm and pulled me to a standstill. "We'll get off the hills, we'll go back, we'll do whatever you need to do, but just take a minute and tell me what that is."

"Okay." I took a deep breath. "Bea was living in New Zealand with her boyfriend, Liam. They were, as far as everyone knew, completely happy. When she arrived back in the UK, I was really surprised. I thought she'd spend the rest of her life with him. She never told anyone why she came home beyond the fact that they'd split up, no details about why they did. But if I look back, that's when she changed. Maybe it was whatever caused the break up that finally pushed her over the edge."

"You think she's killed herself?' Pete looked surprised; it was the first time I'd been willing to concede that Bea might be dead. Even at Albert Road and in Leeds, I'd stuck with vague euphemisms, anything but say the words.

"I hope not but maybe we have to face that. But whatever happened might be linked to Liam in some way. I need to talk to him, see if he can give me any clues." Pete looked sceptical and I saw his point, it must have sounded like a pretty obscure straw to grasp at.

"That was years ago."

"I know, but it's all I've got. I'd better see Caroline and find out what she knows about the breakup. And I'll call

Liam. We should search Bea's house again too when I've spoken to him in case there's something there that I didn't see the significance of. Maybe it's not Whittaker that's the clue, maybe it's what happened in New Zealand?"

"Okay. Let's go."

And we did, hurrying off the mountain. Aware of the steep drops and the loose surface of the path, I followed in Pete's footsteps, half running at times to keep up with his pace, ignoring the pain in muscles that told me to go slower. If I was right and I couldn't help Bea then there was no need to rush, but I wasn't going to waste time admiring the view and enjoying the fresh air.

26

Just a few streets from my parents' home, Caroline opened the door of the house where Bea had grown up, smiled automatically and then looked wary, both wanting and dreading the news I might be bringing.

"Kate, how are you? Do you have—"

'I need to talk to you. I have an idea."

Caroline stepped back and Pete and I went inside. I made brief introductions and she led us through to the kitchen. From force of habit, she clicked the switch on the kettle. Tired, her face drawn, she looked older than when I last saw her a few days earlier. I felt a wave of pity and sympathy, unable to imagine how it must feel to contemplate a future without her only child. I gestured to her to sit down and took the seat opposite her at the table while Pete assumed the tea-making responsibilities.

"Caroline, when Bea came back from New Zealand, do you know what happened between her and Liam? Why did they break up?" I reached across and squeezed her hand. I wished I'd come with good news, any news for that matter, rather than see the disappointment on her face when she realised I had no comfort to offer.

"I've no idea. She would never talk about it." Caroline shrugged and shook her head. "But that was years ago, it can't be relevant to her going off somewhere now, surely?"

"Think about it. When Beatrice met Liam, and when she went to New Zealand with him, she was exactly as she'd always been. Laughing, up for adventure, full of wanderlust. She came back and settled down. She avoided friends, refused to use any social media, withdrew. No-one changes like that unless something big happens, wouldn't you say?"

"I suppose." Caroline sounded doubtful. "I just thought she'd grown up. Bea didn't want to talk about Liam and I hoped that she'd put him behind her and find someone else. I don't think she did though. Only a few dates, as far as I'm aware, but nothing came from them."

"Do you have a phone number for Liam?" I decided to skip past Bea's recent love-life for now.

"Goodness. Somewhere, I suppose. In an old diary or something." Caroline took her tea from Pete and smiled a thank you.

"Could you look for it please? It's important that I contact him."

"Okay." She left the room and Pete looked at me.

"Do you think Liam will talk to you?"

"Who knows? I'm not calling him to cause trouble, I just want to know what happened. Unless he did something dreadful there's no harm in telling me. And we're going to her house to look again for the personal stuff I didn't find the first time. There must be photos and letters, she always used to save that sort of thing and I can't imagine that she'd throw them all away. We'll still go and see Will tomorrow and keep trying to locate Whittaker, but Liam's another angle we need to investigate."

"Sounds like a plan."

"I'm sorry I spoilt our walk."

"It's okay. We'll climb plenty of other mountains, I dare-say. And that one will always be there for us in the future. What matters is Beatrice, right now." He smiled and I felt so grateful that he could help me find Bea, who he'd never even met, without an ounce of resentment that my time and energies were being consumed by her disappearance.

"Here it is." Caroline returned, a slim book in her hand. The writing was small and neat and there were scraps of paper sliding from the pages, new addresses waiting to be written in before the next batch of Christmas cards went out. She pushed it across the table to me, pointing to an address and phone number. "That's Liam and Bea's address and his sister's details next to it. We met when I visited Bea in New Zealand and used to exchange cards. You know, before Beatrice came home."

"Thanks for that." I took a photograph of the two entries. "It's probably nothing, Caroline, it was an idea I had while I was trying to think about where she might have gone or what's triggered her disappearance. The other I want to do is take another look at her house. Can I borrow the key please?"

"Of course." Caroline reached into her handbag, hanging on the back of a chair and I heard the keys jingle as she rooted for them. "Would you like me to come and help you look?"

"It's okay. I need to pop back to Mum and Dad's first. I promise I'll be in touch as soon as I have any news." I drained my tea and stood up to leave, needing to be away from Caroline's almost palpable grief and confusion.

I wished I could ease her pain but all I could do was hug her on the doorstep. At least I had a new idea at last. It might not answer any questions but it was better than simply banging my head against the brick wall of identifying Bea's lover.

WE ARRIVED at Mum and Dad's as they were washing up after lunch, prompting a flurry of concern as to whether we'd eaten and the production of bread and leftover roast beef. I sloped off to the dining room to call Liam, abandoning Pete to Mum's tried-and-tested interrogation method of lulling her victim with food before going in hard with the questions.

I settled myself down at the table, found some paper to make notes, and tried to work out what to say. It was a tricky one because Liam was bound to ask why I needed to know why they split up and 'because I think the trauma of your breakup caused a massive change in Bea's personality and I'm concerned that the ongoing fallout of that has, several years down the line, driven her to suicide' wasn't the ideal response.

In the end, I decided to go with introducing myself, mentioning Bea and gently explaining that we were worried and that it would help to understand why they broke up, even though it was so long ago, just in case it was related.

"Hello." The voice that answered was female and sleepy. I rolled my eyes at myself for not remembering to check time zones. "Natalie speaking."

"Hi. I'm so sorry to wake you, I forgot the time difference. But I wonder if you can help me. My name is Kate Carpenter and I'm calling from England. I'm trying to get hold of Liam Kenwood." I was smiling, light and cheerful, not a hint that this was anything serious.

"I see." The woman paused, and even in those two words, I noted that her tone was less than warm.

"You probably remember my friend Beatrice. They were together for quite a while and I'm attempting to track her down. It might be a shot in the dark, but I was hoping that he'd heard from her recently."

"I'm Liam's sister, Natalie. None of us have had any contact with Bea in years. Liam least of all, I'm afraid." I heard, even on that long-distance line, the faintest quiver in her voice and I hesitated, wondering what it meant. "You see, a week before Bea left to come back to England, Liam killed himself."

"I'm so sorry. I had no idea." My stomach plummeted.

"Bea didn't tell you?" Natalie sounded curious.

"No. She didn't tell anyone. Not even her mother, Caroline. Bea just said they'd split up and she'd decided to return to the UK. It was a surprise because we were all under the impression that they were really happy, but she arrived back without warning or explanation."

"It was a shock to everyone, Bea included." Natalie sighed as though steeling herself to recount the tragic details yet again. "Liam had always tended to get low and from time to time he took anti-depressants. This time, none of us noticed how depressed he was. He'd been hiding it well. And then one day Bea came home from the store and there was a note waiting for her."

"I see."

"We had people out looking for him but it's pretty remote out here and it was a couple of days before anyone found him. He'd gone up in the hills, left the truck and then walked for an hour or two." Her voice cracked but she carried on. "He'd drunk a bottle of whisky, taken a load of pills—sleeping tablets, painkillers and so on. Even capsules of some drug that gets used for date rape. God knows where he got those from."

"I'm so sorry," I repeated. There weren't any other words.

"Bea didn't stay for the funeral. She simply booked a flight and left. At the time I was angry with her but you know, people cope with things in different ways. She wrote to me a few months later, explained that she'd had to go, that she couldn't deal with our grief on top of her own. I replied, told her it was okay and that I understood, but I've never heard from her since. That must be about seven years ago now."

"Something like that." I closed my eyes, my mind filling in the gaps in my knowledge regarding Bea's disappearance, making it all too clear what might have happened.

"But you said you were looking for Bea?"

"Yes." I paused but saw no point in being reticent. "She's gone missing. No-one's seen her for three weeks or so. At first, we assumed she'd just gone on holiday without telling anyone. But it feels less and less like that now. We went to school together and her mum asked me to see if I could find her. Liam was a long shot, but I wondered if there was a clue in how their relationship ended that might tell me where she is."

"You think what happened with Liam is your clue?" Natalie put into words what I was thinking.

"I thought if I knew why they broke up, I might be able to work out what's happened to her. She seemed to change so much when she came back to the UK. Now..."

"Perhaps this also gives you a clue." Natalie's voice was bleak. "But a different one."

"Maybe. It was a trauma that as far as I'm aware, she

never spoke about. Perhaps his suicide affected her more deeply than any of us knew and she decided to take the same way out." I felt cold at the prospect.

"I wouldn't have described Bea as the suicidal type but then again, I'd never thought of Liam like that either."

There was a pause, while I processed that what I'd formerly thought of as an outside chance was now looking a whole lot more probable. I could hear Natalie's sadness in every word and every breath.

"I'm sorry to bring all this up again, Natalie. If I'd had any idea that—"

"It's okay. You weren't to know. Get back to me if I can be of any further use. I mean it, don't worry about upsetting me if it might help you find Beatrice."

"Thanks. That's kind of you."

"Don't worry about it. Liam's gone and we have to do our best to hold onto the living, Kate. They're what matter most."

Going into the kitchen, I was sure I'd composed myself, ready to put an optimistic spin on this and head off, after a snack, to go and search Bea's house again.

When I needed to, during Chris's trial for example, or when Sokolov's thugs trashed my flat, I'd always been able to employ a steely will that kept emotions at bay until I was willing to let them out.

But it seemed I wasn't hiding things as well as I thought and when Pete, halfway through a doorstep of a roast beef sandwich, looked up and I saw the questions in his eyes, I fell apart.

It was the first time I'd let myself cry about Beatrice, the first time I'd allowed the possibilities of what could have happened past my defences, the first time I'd given in to my fear. Even at Albert Road, looking around a dark garden and wondering if she was lying there in a shallow grave, I'd kept it together. But face-to-face with Natalie's grief and the stark awareness that Bea might have chosen to do the same, I lost the ability to just keep on, keeping on.

Brushing away tears, I took a seat at the table, oblivious to my mother's arm around my shoulders, to Pete's hands holding mine, and my dad—bless him—making tea. I don't know how long it was before I managed to pull myself together and come to a hiccupping, sniffing, pause and raise my head again to face their concern.

"Kate, love. What happened?" Mum sat down beside me, a hand rubbing my back, as mothers have always soothed their children, and Dad put a mug down in front of me, in the way that emotionally repressed fathers have always dealt with tears, I suspected.

"You know who I called?" I asked and they nodded, Pete presumably having filled them in while I was on the phone. "That was his sister, Natalie. Bea returned to the UK when Liam—" My lip wobbled again and it was a couple of minutes before I could finish the explanation.

"And you think Beatrice might have done the same?" Mum clarified and I sipped my tea.

"It makes sense, doesn't it?" I asked. "She was never the same after she came back, wouldn't talk about why they split up. Maybe she was hiding her depression and finally decided she wasn't able to go on doing that any longer." The thought that she could have been so desperate and been unable to turn to me for help hit me. I really hadn't been there for her.

"You couldn't have known," said Pete. "People hide this

sort of thing. Even her mother didn't suspect she was having problems."

"Are you going to tell Caroline?" Mum asked.

"No. Not yet. I've got other leads to follow up before I come to any conclusions that I need to share with her. If I'm wrong, and obviously I hope I am, I don't want to break her heart unnecessarily."

"So what's next?" Mum was always practical. "If you really do think she's killed herself, perhaps you should call the police."

"I know."

"You wanted to go through her house again. We should do that first," Pete said. "And tomorrow you can visit Will's office and see if that gets us anywhere. If he has a lead on Whittaker, then we'll follow that up. If he has nothing, then we should talk to Caroline and call the cops." Pete was calm and practical, exactly what I needed now that those qualities had deserted me.

"Good plan. Let's get going. I want to look everywhere in her house. Somewhere there must be a clue." I sighed, drained. My peaceful, happy moment on the mountain felt like a lifetime ago. For a while, I'd been optimistic about finding Bea, sure that all I needed was the information that would lead me to Whittaker and I'd find her. That confidence was fading fast.

27

We drove to Bea's in near silence. I gave Pete directions but couldn't manage conversation as I willed myself to be capable, practical, unemotional. In some ways, I wished I hadn't called Liam's family and instead just concentrated on hunting down Whittaker in the hope that even if he didn't lead me to Bea, at least I'd have enough to force the police to take action. Then I could wait for them to come to me with news, a layer of protection between me and the raw truth of Bea's disappearance.

And what had happened? I'd originally been sure that Bea was inconsiderate, then that she'd run off with her lover. Now, I had to add in the possibility that he might have killed her, or that she'd possibly taken her own life. More options, more endings, few of them good.

"You okay?" Pete parked outside Bea's house and looked across at me.

"Yes. I mean, no. But I don't have a choice in the matter. Come on." I got out of the car and walked slowly up the path. Since my first visit, a few days earlier, the garden had grown a little more spring-like, even more daffodils raising cheerful faces to the sun and wind. Other than that, everything looked much the same. Certainly, Bea still wasn't waving to me from the sitting room window which was all I wanted to see.

It seemed Caroline hadn't been to the house since she came with me and I scooped up a handful of mail from the mat. I flicked through it—council tax, a reminder regarding car servicing, a load of junk leaflets. No bank statements, nothing personal, nothing useful. I chucked it on the pile on the dining table and took some latex gloves from my bag, handing a pair to Pete.

"Just in case."

"Where shall we start and what are we looking for?" He snapped the gloves on and looked expectant.

"Personal stuff. Last time I was here, it surprised me how impersonal everything was. Nothing that gave me an insight into Bea's private life or her state of mind. Save for the phone and diary, obviously, which she either forgot or left behind because she didn't think anyone could glean anything from them. And the naughty knicker drawer. At first, it amused me because it seemed so incongruous. Now, with all the secrecy, and the tone of his texts telling her what to wear and to send him photos, it backs up my conviction that he was controlling. And that can escalate fast."

"Her lingerie shows that he's controlling?" Pete raised an eyebrow.

"Possibly. Remember, I've known her a long time and I don't think she's the kinky undies type. The odd suspender belt is one thing, but this was another level. To me, it implies he was quite insistent that she fit in with his tastes."

"I see. I didn't realise there was such a subtext. I'll remember that when I shop for your Christmas present."

"Buying lingerie is not a gift for me. It's a treat for you, darling." I smiled, despite everything. "Come on, you start with the sitting room. Anything that might tell us what her plans were. Any plans at all. I didn't know what I was looking for last time and I might have missed something."

"It's very tidy." Pete looked around the dining room with its alphabetised bookshelves and bland artwork.

"It is. And her departure looks planned. The fridge is empty, she took the bins out and so on. If you're so low that you're planning to end it all, do you worry about those things? It's more like she was going on holiday, but she didn't mention taking a trip to anyone. And if she's been abducted, it was by someone who returned to tidy up."

"If Whittaker harmed her, he might have come back to clean house," Pete suggested, voicing the fear I couldn't.

"I know. If we don't get anywhere tomorrow after we've been to see Will, we'll come back with a UV light and luminol. See what those show. I'm sure I can get hold of some. If we find anything then the police will have to take this seriously. I didn't do that at first because I thought she'd just gone off of her own volition, but we'll have to consider the worst-case scenarios."

. "I think so."

"And there's the phone. Did she forget it? Or did she not need it any more because she wasn't intending to be in touch with Whittaker again? Or maybe he missed it when he was cleaning up?" I sighed and shook my head. "So for now, we search. And everything we find that might tell us anything we put to one side to go through later. Do you want to check downstairs?"

"I'm certainly not going near her bedroom." Pete glanced around. "How thorough? Carpets up?"

"If you think something might be underneath. Check

under the sofa and so on, behind the bookcases, under the kitchen cupboards. Notebooks, receipts, that sort of thing."

I left him to it and went upstairs, starting with the main bathroom, only this time I didn't just search the medicine cabinet but took out my mini toolkit and unscrewed the bath panel.

There was nothing there save a few offcuts of plastic pipe so I fixed it back in place. In the small bedroom that served as her wardrobe overflow, I checked the pockets of the clothes hanging there, every inch of the built-in wardrobe, under the mattress of the spare bed, and ran my hands across the carpet in case anything had been slid out of sight. Nothing.

Going through to Bea's en-suite bathroom, I took out the medication in the wall cupboard. The same things as I'd seen before but this time I read the chemist's label on one of the boxes. Some sort of strong painkiller, I thought. 50mg, dated about a week before Bea vanished. I opened it and pulled out a single blister pack containing twelve tablets. I looked again at the box; there had been over a hundred in here to start with. According to the label that was six weeks' supply. If Bea had taken them with her, she must have planned to be away for a while. Or had she just grabbed a handful to take with her, part of her plan to end it all?

Rummaging through the rest of the meds, I couldn't find anything else of concern. I chucked the little white box to one side and started to look around Bea's room again. Nothing hidden in the wardrobe, nor beneath the mattress or the carpet or the rug. Nothing taped beneath the bedside tables or the chest of drawers. Nothing among her clothes or beneath the paper lining of the drawers. I pulled open the drawers beneath the divan bed again. Three were empty, one contained the lingerie that her lover seemed so keen on.

This time, I rummaged through it, wondering if something was concealed, and heard the thud of something heavy in the bottom. I found a clear glass bottle, about 50ml or so, and looked at it in confusion. Perfume? Unscrewing the top, I sniffed but it was odourless. I put the top back on and added it to the box of tablets. What could it be and why was it hidden?

"ANY LUCK?" Pete was working through the bookcases when I went downstairs, shaking each book to see if there was anything loose tucked inside.

"Maybe. Natalie said that Liam took a load of pills when he—" I suddenly struggled to say the words. "I found an almost empty box of meds and this bottle was hidden away." I put them both on the coffee table.

"Can you tell what's in the bottle?" Pete asked and I shook my head.

"No smell and I'm not about to taste it. But it was in what you charmingly refer to as the naughty knicker drawer so it's something she wanted to keep out of sight."

"Anna or Olly might be able to identify it," he suggested.

"I thought that. And they'll know whether these are meds you could do yourself harm with." Again, hedging around the words. "Come on. Let's go."

Back in the car, I looked back at Bea's house, neat and tidy like all the others in the street, and I wished it could tell me the secrets I was sure it still held.

. . .

At Anna and Olly's house, it was the children's bedtime and I resigned myself to an impatient hour or so before they would be in bed and I could reasonably produce the possibly illegal and dangerous medications. But I'd forgotten that Pete was a novelty and Alice and Jack dragged him off, spotting him as a mark who'd be susceptible to pleas for 'just one more story'.

In the kitchen, Olly opened a bottle of wine and settled himself on a bar stool, looking expectant.

"How's it going?"

"Not well." I filled him and Anna in on the day's revelations and laid the packet of pills and the bottle of clear liquid on the worktop in front of them. "Tell me about these. What's in the bottle? And how many of those tablets would it take to kill you?"

"We do have the cheeriest conversations." Anna looked at the box. "They're opioids. Strong ones that you'd prescribe for severe, long-term pain, like a bad back. The sort of thing your friend the other night was taking. I'd only give a patient these if they'd been having problems for a while and other meds and physiotherapy hadn't worked. To overdose, probably a few dozen to be sure of doing the job. Chuck in some alcohol, maybe some antidepressants or sleeping pills and you'd be certain." I bit my lip to stop it wobbling and she reached out to stroke my arm. "I'm sorry, Kate."

"No, it's fine. Good to know. And that stuff?" I pointed at the bottle and Olly, an A&E doctor, picked it up, unscrewed the lid and sniffed it just as I had. Then he dipped his finger in and touched it to his tongue, pulling a face.

"Odourless, bit salty. GHB, I'd say." I must have looked blank. "It can be used as a date-rape drug. Like Rohypnol. We see it occasionally in A&E."

"What the fuck would Bea be doing with that?" Anna asked.

"I don't know. Nothing good." Olly pulled a rueful face and shrugged. "You wouldn't want to take it with those painkillers. Not a good combination."

"At least she didn't take it with her." That was a relief.

"She wouldn't need much and it's only half full. She could have decanted a bit. How did Liam kill himself?"

"Pain meds, sleeping tablets, whisky." I paused. "And some Rohypnol. Maybe he used that to take away the fear, the awareness of what he was going to do." I closed my eyes, memories of Bea as a laughing teenager, my best friend, dancing before my eyes. "She's done it, hasn't she?" I felt a weight descend upon my shoulders, tears welling.

"She might not have. Not yet. There may still be time." But even Anna didn't sound convinced of that.

"Possibly. But I don't think so. I expect we're now looking for her body." And my head dropped forward as tears fell, keening, wracking sobs that shook me. I was aware of Anna's arms around me, but I couldn't stop, lost in the horror of what might have happened and guilt that I hadn't known or been able to prevent it.

THAT EVENING, while Pete cooked supper, one eye keeping watch over me, I skimmed through the text messages between Whittaker and Bea. When I'd read them before, I was looking for the details that would help me identify the mystery man and locate Beatrice. Now, the tone and subtext of their messages took on a new significance.

Bea was gushing and adoring but although Whittaker was ostensibly similarly romantic, I saw disconcerting aspects. It was clear that their relationship was run along the lines he dictated from the way he told her what to wear, to the location of their meetings—always at a venue of his choosing. I'd skipped over it before but it seemed that one night she'd gone out with colleagues from work, a birthday dinner, and that had irked him because he thought she might be meeting another man.

That last struck home. I remembered how Chris would question my whereabouts, insisting that a delayed flight was a fiction I'd invented to cover up my infidelity. He'd ranted at me while I waited in an American departure lounge hiding my tears from fellow passengers as I tried to pacify him.

I eventually got home and told him when he came to my flat that it was over, which was when he attacked me. I went cold imagining Bea standing up to Whittaker like that. How would he have reacted given that I already saw signs of coercion?

Although Whittaker used all the right words and I genuinely believed that he wanted to be free of his wife so he could be with Beatrice, his tone was more clinical and less sentimental than hers. I got the feeling that she saw the two of them as star-crossed lovers, kept apart by circumstance but united in their wish that things could be different.

Conversely, while he seemed to see his wife as a barrier to their happiness, I also saw that it was a useful way to keep stringing Bea along, promising the moon but always having an excuse to hide behind.

The tone of their texts changed a little a couple of weeks before Bea disappeared and it sounded, reading them again, like they'd been plotting something, although it was impossible to know what. Even a weekend away seemed to require MI6-level planning to line up alibis and excuses.

In that last fortnight, there had been talk of plans, of

escape, of needing to keep things quiet and I wondered whether they'd been going to run away. Maybe they were at this very minute drinking cocktails on a beach somewhere, thinking how clever they were.

I didn't like that duplicity and callousness, but the other options were too painful to contemplate. That Whittaker might have broken Bea's heart, leaving her so bereft and alone that she'd killed herself. Or perhaps these drugs had nothing to do with it. Perhaps she'd threatened to reveal all to Whittaker's wife and he'd gone from controlling to violent.

I remembered, shivering, how Chris had grabbed me by the throat when he assaulted me and how I'd blacked out after fighting him as long as I could. I never let myself think about the 'what-ifs', but what if Whittaker hadn't walked away in time.

"You okay there?" Pete kissed the top of my head and placed a glass of wine in front of me as he sat down at the table.

"Not really. But tomorrow's going to be productive, if nothing else, I think. At least we can find things to rattle and see what shakes loose." I tried to smile. "I'm sorry I spoiled your day in the hills."

"It doesn't matter. We have plenty of time for more mountains." He leaned in to kiss me and I closed my eyes, letting myself feel loved and cared for.

Tomorrow was another day. Tomorrow we would once again keep on, keeping on.

28

I barely slept that night, impatient at the prospect of going to Will's office as soon as it opened and extracting information about the man he'd recognised with Beatrice at Charlecote Manor. Churning through a hundred possible scenarios in my mind, I tossed and turned until I finally gave up before dawn and started picking my way around the bedroom in darkness, trying to find my running kit.

"What are you doing?" Pete clicked on the bedside lamp and blinked at me in the light.

"Going for a run. I can't sleep."

"It's six am. Not even properly light." He ran a hand through his fair hair and yawned.

"You of all people should be used to early mornings." I grinned. "Go to sleep. I'll be back in an hour or so."

"I'll come with you." He rolled out of bed and opened a drawer.

"It's fine. I'm okay on my own."

"I'm awake now. And I could do with the exercise. Unless you just want to come back to bed?" His eyes twinkled in the dimness of the room and I was tempted, but only for a second.

"No, I'm too restless. I'll warn you though, I'm not going slowly on your account."

"The day I can't keep up with you, I'll return my medals."

WE RAN FOR SEVERAL MILES, falling into step beside each other along roads I remembered well, then along the riverbank and up to the Ketch Inn before turning back and coasting down the long slope of the Bath Road before heading across towards Fort Royal, from where Charles the First commanded his troops.

Pausing in the park on top of the hill, I pointed this out to Pete. For a moment he looked interested by this fun military factoid, then, getting his bearings, he turned for home without warning, increasing his pace so that I had to sprint to catch him.

Threading our way through the almost deserted early morning streets of the city centre, each pushing the other to go faster, by the time we got back to his cottage my lungs were burning. I flopped onto a garden bench to recover.

"Thought you'd be quicker than me, eh?" Pete sat beside me and put an arm round my shoulders, pulling me close to kiss me. He'd passed through the gate about half a yard ahead of me.

"Not really. I just like to keep you on your toes." I smiled, pleased at having pushed my whirling feelings of guilt, anxiety and impatience from my mind for a while.

. . .

We arrived at Jeffries, Gardner and Co. shortly after nine. At first, the receptionist tried to fob us off with, "I'll see if Mr Jeffries is available" but I was in no mood to be patient.

"If Will's here, he's available," I told her in my best no-nonsense voice. "Tell him it's Kate Carpenter and I need to talk to him about his visit to Charlecote Manor."

"Very well." Looking uncertain, she disappeared through a door at the back of the office.

"Now, try not to rip his head off if he can't tell you what you want to know," Pete whispered.

"Why?" I asked. "If he won't help then he's just collateral damage, surely?"

"Would you like to come through?" The receptionist reappeared and ushered us through to Will's office. He was standing up, his usual estate agent bonhomie tempered by a wariness in his eyes.

"Kate, so lovely to see you. It's been absolutely years, isn't it? Must have been our wedding. Sophie, could you bring us coffee, please?" He still had some of the boyish charm I remembered, albeit with a slightly receding hairline and a waistline that was starting to betray the number of business lunches he enjoyed.

"No thanks," I told Sophie. "Will, this isn't a social call and I'm not in the market for a barn conversion."

"I see." Sophie left and Will gestured us to a couple of chairs, looking questioningly at Pete. I sighed, not in the mood for niceties. "Will, this is Pete Alderton. Pete, this is Will Jeffries. He's currently sleeping with his wife's best friend and a few weeks ago they bumped into Beatrice and her mystery lover. Joanna tells me that Will knows who that man was and Will's now going to tell us." My tone was conversational and, introductions over, I turned back to Will and raised an expectant eyebrow. "Well?"

"I'm not sure what you're talking about." He tried to force a laugh, looking from one to the other of us, but neither Pete nor I were smiling.

"Rubbish." I couldn't be bothered with this time-wasting. "You know exactly what I'm talking about. When you were having an illicit lunch with Joanna at Charlecote Manor you saw Beatrice Copley with a man she's been having an affair with. You recognised him. Bea's gone missing and I need you to confirm that man's identity and tell me where to find him. It's really very simple."

"Bea's not missing. You're over-reacting. She's probably just on holiday." Will tried to bat away my request with a sneering dismissal that I didn't appreciate.

"Trust me, she's not on holiday, Will. Who was he?"

"I can't tell you. It would be very indiscreet. He's married." He was blustering, playing for time.

"So are you."

"Even so—"

"Tell me who he is, Will." I sighed. "Otherwise, I'm going to go straight round to your house and inform Susie that you've been shagging Joanna. And I'll tell Joanna's husband the same thing. I'm not so bothered about being discreet, you see. I just want to find Bea." I looked at him coldly, not a flicker of warmth on my face or in my voice. Will flicked a glance towards Pete sitting beside me, legs crossed patiently, two fingers tapping on the arm of the chair, a little intimidating even while being perfectly polite.

"You're just causing trouble." Will was starting to get cross as he realised he was trapped. "There's no need to tell them."

"You're right, there's no need. But I will if you don't give me the information I want." I kept my voice even. "Is it really worth bringing all that down on yourself simply to protect this man's anonymity? What do you owe him?"

"Nothing, I suppose. But professional courtesy—"

"Please, Will." I cut across his prevarications. "I'm worried and I have to find her. This man is the best lead I've got. Never mind how you'll feel if I blow your world apart, imagine how you'll feel if something happens to Bea and being straight with me would have prevented it."

"Well, maybe." Will dithered, flicking through the pages of his diary. "And you swear you won't breathe a word to Susie?"

"I'm promising nothing, not at this stage. If the police get involved it may all come out but I don't see the point of making people unhappy if it isn't necessary."

"If Susie finds out, I'll blame you." Will hesitated.

"I can live with that." I shrugged, uninterested in his marriage or its future.

"Fine. His name's Jeremy Whittaker."

"Jeremy? He gave his name as Jonathan to an hotel."

"He must have used a false name. He's definitely called Jeremy. I used to play rugby against him at school."

"Okay. Tell me about him."

"I haven't seen him for months. Even at Charlecote we didn't chat. He's a nice bloke though. Married and I don't think he's got any kids. Wife's rather difficult, I believe. Highly strung. You know the type. He lives in Birmingham —Solihull, I think, or Edgbaston. He's a developer with fingers in a lot of pies. He puts a fair bit of business my way and I wouldn't want to upset him, Kate."

"I have no intention of upsetting anyone if I can avoid it. I just need to find Beatrice. I'll need his address."

"Really? You can't turn up there. What about his wife?"

Will looked aghast, probably imagining the horror of that happening to him.

"I won't go there unless I have to. If you give me his number I'll try calling first. But I'd better have all the information now." I leaned back in my chair, making myself comfortable. "It might take you a few minutes to find it, but that's okay. I can wait."

There was a pause, just a few seconds, while Will looked at me and I could practically hear his brain whirring as he considered possible outcomes. Then, obviously deciding that keeping me happy was the best way to avoid chaos in his own life, he pressed a buzzer and asked Sophie to come back through. After five minutes of rather stilted small talk while she found the details, I had Whittaker's home address on a post-it.

"What do you think has happened to Beatrice?" Will sounded more concerned, perhaps realising that I wouldn't go to these lengths unless I was worried.

"I'm not sure. But I've seen their texts and Whittaker unsettles me." I forced a polite smile. "Thanks for your help, Will. The sooner I can find her and check she's okay, the sooner I can go home to Edinburgh and my own life."

"Well, good luck. But promise me you'll be discreet. He won't want this getting back to his wife."

"No Will, he probably doesn't." I got to my feet and Pete followed suit. "It's a pity that those who'd rather their spouses didn't find out they've been playing around don't just, you know, avoid playing around? Maybe you should try that."

Pete opened the door for me and on the threshold I paused. Will looked uncomfortable, plucking at his tie.

"Bye, Kate."

"Bye. Thanks for this. If I need more info I'll be in touch."

And we left, a scrap of paper with the information I'd been after for so long in my hand at last.

"I'm impressed. You got what you wanted and made him feel like a complete heel at the same time. Good work." Pete smiled as we stood outside on the pavement.

"Thank you. It's a useful skill, I find." I looked at the details Will had given us. "We won't call him. We'll go and scope out the house first. I'm sure I can think up a cover story if I need to. Let's get going."

29

Whittaker's house wasn't dissimilar to the one on Albert Road that we'd checked out a few nights ago, just half a mile away. It had a bit less footballer-bling and the gates were old and wrought iron, standing open as they probably had for years, rather than silently sliding electric ones but in general, it was the same type of large detached place that had filled this suburb for over a century, housing the middle classes behind their ornate woodwork, sash windows and neat shrubberies. There was a for sale sign attached to the railings.

We clocked the house number and did two laps of the block, passing slowly enough that we could get an idea of the lie of the land, but not so much that we'd arouse suspicion. It looked perfectly normal. Pete pulled into a space about fifty yards down the street.

"Right, you stay here and I'll go and see what we're dealing with." I undid my seatbelt and he caught my arm.

"Seriously? You think I'm about to let you walk in there alone?"

"Yes. I'll be fine. He's probably not there, just his wife.

I'm only going to get whoever opens the door talking, see if I can glean any information. It isn't my intention to kick off with 'where's my friend, you murdering bastard', you know."

"No."

"No? Are you forbidding me to go on my own?" Even I could hear the warning note in my voice. I hoped Pete did too.

"I'm not happy about you doing this alone. You have no idea what you're walking into." Pete still had hold of my arm and I could see the concern on his face.

"Okay. Look, the for sale sign makes it easy. Unless Bea opens the door, and I doubt she will, I'll make out I'm looking for a house round here. My husband's job means we're relocating, that sort of thing. That story usually works. Give me fifteen minutes and come and look for me. You can pretend to be my husband. If it's all completely innocent, we won't have alarmed his wife unnecessarily, but if it turns out he's got Bea held hostage in the house, then you're only a few minutes behind me and you're welcome to deal with it as you see fit." Pete still didn't look convinced. "Look, if I knew Bea was definitely in there, I'd have you scramble some former comrades and we'd storm the place like it was a besieged embassy. But as we know so little, this is really just a fishing expedition to find out what's going on."

"Ten minutes." Pete still didn't look happy.

"Fifteen." He countered.

"Twelve."

"Done."

"Be careful." Pete released my arm and squeezed my hand. "Stay outside if you can and if you have to go in, don't let anyone get between you and the exit. Ideally, no further than the hallway and make sure the front door stays open."

When Pete and I worked together to recover a painting I would have spent months tracking it down but I was happy for the actual recovery to happen on his terms. We also usually had help with us in the form of other ex-military types and a reasonable arsenal of weapons.

Walking in there, alone and unarmed, was something Pete would feel pretty relaxed about, given that he has training most people don't. But being nosy, asking questions, and adopting a cover story in order to gather information was how I worked. I could see why he thought it might be reckless but it was the only way to do it.

Like I said, this was Monday morning in a Birmingham suburb, not Kabul, and this was a messy domestic situation, not a hostage rescue operation.

I PLAYED MY PART WELL. I looked from the for sale sign to the red-brick house, smiling at its gables and arched windows like a house hunter who'd struck gold. Fiddling with my phone, taking a couple of pictures, I faffed around long enough that anyone inside would see me as unthreatening. Then, slightly hesitantly, with an awkward smile and a bit of hair-fiddling, I walked past a very shiny Range Rover to the door, pulled the brass handle, and heard a bell jangling somewhere deep in the house.

The man who opened the door was instantly recognisable as Jeremy Whittaker, better looking in the flesh than in the photographs I'd found. Tall, fair hair, startling blue eyes and, I noticed, as he looked me up and down, assessing, the easy smile of the habitual philanderer.

"Hi," I began. "I know this is dreadfully cheeky but my husband and I are relocating and house-hunting in the area. Yours looks perfect but I can't get through to the agent and I wondered whether you might have a copy of the sales particulars that I could take away." I gave him my most charming smile, head slightly tilted to one side to look even less threatening.

"I'm sure we do. Come in, I'll dig a copy out for you." He stepped back, inviting me inside and, unable to refuse without seeming rude and possibly arousing suspicion, I followed, just into the hallway. "Where are you moving from?"

"London. My husband's taking a job at the university. It's a lovely house. Are you going far?"

"Overseas. France, maybe. We just need to sort out paperwork. I'm looking forward to a change, you know?"

He waited, smiling, while I looked around the hall; high ceilings, lots of ornate Victorian plasterwork, photos on the wall, and a pile of 'with deepest sympathy' cards on a side table. I let him see me spot them and fought to hide my realisation that this might be about to play out contrary to all the outcomes I'd considered.

"I'm so sorry, is this a bad time?" I waved in the direction of the cards. "I feel dreadful for crashing in like this."

"It's fine." Whittaker made as if to lay a hand on my arm but pulled back as though he'd thought better of it. "My wife had been unwell for years. It was inevitable really."

"I'm terribly sorry for your loss. I should go." I took a step towards the door, smile still in place but more sympathetic now. My brain was whirring.

"Thanks. But it was a few weeks ago and it's getting easier. The initial shock's passed, you know? That's why I've decided to move. It's just me rattling around with my memories and it's time for a fresh start. Wait here, I'll get those particulars."

Whittaker's expression was a careful portrayal of loss

tempered with show-must-go-on stoicism and I didn't believe a word of it.

He disappeared down the hallway to the back of the house leaving me near the slightly ajar front door while I worked out the possibilities. Part of me wanted to flee but I needed more information. A few more minutes of polite chat and I might have something I could take to the police.

His wife was dead. I hadn't considered that possibility for more than a fleeting second. From the way he talked about her in his texts to Beatrice, I'd got the impression that his wife was very convenient for him. He could fool around with other women but if they became serious and wanted more, then he could remind them of her fragility and that he could never leave her. He could insist that he'd always been very clear about that.

Her death left the way open for Bea and him to be together. When I'd thought that he might have murdered Bea, my own experience with a controlling partner had obviously skewed my judgement and made me too quick to fear the worst when I saw those signs in his behaviour. But I hadn't even considered this.

I heard a floorboard creak upstairs and footsteps. He wasn't rattling around this house all alone, as he'd said. Someone was up there and I could guess who.

"Kate, could you just come through here for a moment?"

"Okay." Caught off-guard, distracted by the realisation that Bea was almost certainly in the house, my response was automatic and as soon as I spoke I knew I'd made a mistake.

Whittaker appearing, coming back up the hall towards me, moving fast, something in his hand. I stepped back, stumbled on a rug and my shoulder shoved the front door shut behind me.

"That was careless, wasn't it, Kate?" His friendly if rueful smile was gone, replaced by something far colder. He was ten feet from me, a gap too easy for him to close in a second.

"How did you guess my name? I didn't introduce myself." Maybe I could convince him that it was a coincidence and I really was a house hunter called Kate. After all, it wasn't an unusual name. I slid my hand into my shoulder bag, reaching for something to help me.

"You didn't need to. Bea had photos of the two of you in her house. You've changed a bit over the last few years but you're still recognisable."

"Where is Bea?"

"Why did you come looking for her?" He took a step closer.

"Her mother asked me to. She's worried about her. And I am too." I couldn't find the pepper spray in my bag but my hand closed around something else.

"She's fine. And now that Alison is dead, Bea and I can be together. We're going to the continent and we'll start again." His tone was smug, as though his plan had worked perfectly and I was a mere fly in the ointment.

"How did your wife die?" I edged nearer to the door but he closed the gap a little more.

"I'm sure you know how." He shrugged. "You're bright, Bea tells me. I'm sure you've sussed it out by now."

"You killed her." My right hand found the door handle behind my back, out of his sight.

"It's called assisted suicide." He looked unconcerned, a psychopath without empathy who could bend any fact to suit the story he'd decided to tell. And who wanted to brag about how clever he'd been. "She'd been threatening to do it for years."

"Did she want you to assist her? Because if she didn't it's

just common-or-garden murder." I began to turn the doorknob, praying it didn't stick or squeak.

"She's not here to say otherwise, is she? As far as the doctors are concerned it was suicide. Up in the hills, a lonely spot, pills and a bottle of vodka beside her. I made it look exactly right. And of course her history of mental illness. A classic scenario, wouldn't you say?" He smiled, pleased he'd pulled off this perfect murder. "Come away from that door."

"No." My hand was still on the doorknob and he reached out, grabbing my bag, yanking it off my shoulder and throwing it across the hall. I backed up to the door again.

"Move." And that's when I saw the knife he was holding, a heavy kitchen knife with a ten-inch blade, catching the light from the leaded glass either side of the front door. Not something I wanted anywhere near me.

I could deal with the knife myself or try delaying tactics, hoping my twelve minutes was up and that my cavalry was about to arrive. Remembering something Pete told me about being captured—play for time, keep them talking, trust that help is on its way—I hoped he was right. I had more confidence in my gift of the gab than in my ability to disarm Whittaker.

"No." I repeated. "You don't want to hurt me, Jeremy. At the moment, everyone thinks Alison killed herself. If anything happens to me then you'll have a lot of explaining to do. And how will Bea feel? Knowing that you hurt her friend?"

I kept my voice calm, trying to seem reasonable while my right hand still worked on the door handle. At last, I felt it loosen, free of the catch. I slid the snib down, preventing the door latching again.

"She'll understand. Bea wants to be with me." Jeremy

spoke in a tone that couldn't comprehend that Bea would have any sense of guilt or loyalty to anyone else.

"But at that cost? I don't think so. She's clever. If you hurt me she'll know that you're not to be trusted." Surely Pete should be here by now? Every second I stood there, trying to look Whittaker in the eye without losing sight of that wicked blade, dragged by like an eternity. "Let me see Bea, see that she's safe and I'll walk away and leave you alone. I'll be able to tell her mother she's okay, even if she's not coming home."

"That would be useful." Whittaker looked thoughtful, as though weighing up pros and cons and I moved sideways, ready to throw open the door and run.

"It's the best option for everyone."

"But you could talk. You strike me as someone who'd talk." And he lunged at me, the blade flashing as it came towards me.

30

I dodged to the side and flicked out the telescopic baton I'd sneaked out of my bag, striking Whittaker's knife hand and inflicting enough shock and pain that he dropped the knife and it skittered away across the tiled floor.

Ignoring his roar of anger, I threw open the door and fled, taking the steps in one stride, skidding on the gravel as I rounded the gate pier and sprinting down the pavement towards Pete's car. I couldn't hear Whittaker behind me, but I wasn't about to ease up. My fingers fumbled for a second with the door handle and then I was inside.

"Drive!" I yelled. "Just drive."

Pete did, pulling out into the suburban street as soon as the engine caught and I grabbed his mobile from the dash, mine being in my bag somewhere in the hall of Whittaker's house.

"What happened? Are you okay?"

"I'm fine. He faked his wife's suicide and he's got a knife. Bea's inside." With shaking fingers I tapped in 999.

"He didn't hurt you?" Pete took a left, then another,

driving round the block while I tried to explain calmly to the emergency operator what had occurred, keeping it to the shortest, most pertinent details: address, a man with a knife, confessed to killing his wife, tried to stab me, another person still inside, possibly a hostage. I hung up, assured that someone would be here as a matter of urgency, and looked out of the window as Pete pulled up outside Whittaker's house.

"There, on the drive." I pointed and we saw Whittaker hurling belongings into his car. And Beatrice; standing on the front steps looking bewildered.

Mounting the pavement, Pete parked across the driveway, and we watched as Whittaker turned to look at us and realised his escape was blocked. He bent and I saw a flash of silver as he picked up the knife lying on the gravel at his feet. Pete hit the central locking button, but instead of approaching us, Whittaker made a run for it, nipping through the gap between the car and the gate post and setting off up the road, knife in hand.

Pete swore under his breath as he opened the car door.

"I'll stop him. You keep an eye on Bea. Don't let her do a runner as well."

We got out and as I kept Bea in my peripheral vision, I watched Pete sprint after Whittaker, gaining on him quickly. Knowing that Pete was easily the favourite, and shutting out the fear that Whittaker might manage to use his knife, I turned towards Beatrice.

From a distance of about ten yards we looked at each other. My mind was full of images from our youth; picnicking in the Cathedral gardens after our GCSE exams, drinking Pimm's at summer barbecues, passing notes in a Latin lesson when we were twelve, and reading a magazine discreetly in Maths when we were a few years older rather than tackling trigonometry.

I recalled crying in the cloakroom over a boy who'd dumped me and Bea making me giggle as she detailed all the ways in which he wasn't worthy of me. I remembered our abortive trip to Glastonbury when her never-reliable Ford Fiesta gave up the ghost before we'd even got to Cheltenham. More than anything, I remembered us laughing.

And now she stood before me, someone who had doubtless colluded with and assisted Whittaker in the murder of his wife, who'd let what should have been no more than a flirtation become a twisted affair that paid no attention to right or wrong, morally or legally.

Bea might have believed every word he'd told her, every promise he'd made, but surely at some point she must have realised what was happening? Either way, she was someone with whom I would never again laugh until we cried and our sides ached.

"You found me, then," she said, her voice flat.

"Looks like it." I stood facing her with my hands in my pockets, so much to say that I didn't know where to start.

"How?"

"You left your phone behind. I got someone to hack into it and followed the trail. And Joanna was panicking that you might tell her husband you'd seen her with Will and so she made a silly mistake. And your lover didn't give as fictional an address as he thought to an hotel. Lots of fragments of information led me here."

"How clever you are." There was an acid note in her voice.

"And how bloody stupid you've been, Bea." My voice rose, anger coursing through me. She didn't answer, just looked at me, expressionless. "I thought you could be dead. Because you'd been seen there, I searched the garden of that house in Albert Road, wondering if I might find your body. We ended up in a derelict pub in Leeds and found a corpse. For a bit, until a sodding pathologist arrived, I thought it might be you. After I spoke to Liam's family and found the meds at your place I wondered if you'd killed yourself. Your mother is terrified, thinking the worst. And all the time, you were here with him."

"I was perfectly safe with Jeremy." Her tone was defensive.

"Really? Did you see him try to fucking stab me? And now he's run off down the road with a knife in his hand. He's admitted to me that he killed his wife. You actually think you're safe with him? That he wouldn't get rid of you if he saw you as an inconvenience, just like his wife? Don't be an idiot." Angry, shaking with rage, I turned, lashing out with my booted foot and leaving a satisfying dent in the door of Whittaker's Range Rover.

"If you'd ever been in love, you'd know how I feel." Bea shrugged, her expression a little smug despite her world falling apart around her. "You've always been more interested in your career and that's why you'll end up alone. I love him in a way you'll never understand. I'd do anything for him."

"You're right. I don't get it. Loving someone doesn't mean you have to sign up to their warped perception of the world." I heard sirens in the distance and saw Beatrice tense, as though she was thinking of running away. "Stay there. I've run far enough today and I'm not in the mood for it. You can explain to the nice police officers who are about to turn up that your feelings for Jeremy mean that the rule of law doesn't apply to you. They're going to enjoy hearing all about that."

"Jeremy loves me. We'll protect each other." Bea's voice was defiant.

"No. He'll drop you in it. Just wait and see. By the time you sit down in that interview room, he'll have told them it was some weird Fatal Attraction thing and that you killed Alison. If he thinks he can save himself he'll let you take all the blame."

"You're lying."

"I'll bet you anything you like that he'll do exactly that. Your seedy affair is over now and the only value you have to him is if he can make you the scapegoat."

The sirens were growing louder and hearing a crunch of gravel, I turned as the two men returned. Pete had one of Whittaker's arms twisted behind his back, a hand on his shoulder threatening to dislocate it if he struggled. Pete didn't look happy. His right eye was reddened as though Whittaker had got a lucky punch in but more worrying was the bloodstain on his thigh.

"Pete, are you okay?" I didn't want to move nearer in case Bea tried to run.

"Yes. It's just a scratch, I've had worse." His voice was tight, although with pain or anger I wasn't sure, and I saw him jerk Whittaker's arm, making him wince. "Don't worry. The knife's in my back pocket. Take it out and put it on the ground." Without taking my eyes off Bea, I did as he said, chucking the weapon a couple of yards away as I heard tyres squealing outside.

"Armed police! Hands where we can see them!" The air was suddenly full of shouting police officers pointing guns at us, aggressive and assertive, the mention of knives and potential hostages having elicited quite a spectacular response. We did as we were told, waiting for calm so that we could begin what was going to be a long session of explanations.

Pete and I looked at each other, relieved and resigned, and I managed a small, rather grim, smile. Whittaker was furious, already demanding a lawyer and shouting his protests that this was a mix-up, that my accusations were the product of a deranged obsession.

And as she was cuffed and led to a squad car, Bea looked stunned as if only now did she realise that this was not a case of passionate love conquering all. She was safe, my job was done, but her life was never going to be the same again.

31

It was just as I thought; Liam's suicide had provided a template, although rather than Bea using the same method to take her own life, she and Whittaker used it as the model to murder Alison. Bea procured the GHB, goodness knows how, and both of them stocked up on painkillers. A couple of repeat prescriptions from less than attentive GPs and they were able to lay hands on enough opiates to fell an elephant.

Whittaker and his wife went hill-walking, aiming to picnic at a pre-arranged, out of the way location where Bea was lurking. He drugged Alison and, with Bea's help, moved her to a more hidden spot so she wouldn't be found for a while. While she was drugged and compliant, they got her to drink half a bottle of vodka and take a load of painkillers, topped off with a handful of her own sleeping pills for good measure.

Then they waited until she'd drifted off, arranged the scene, and left her to die in the hills on her own. The tablets, drugs and alcohol did most of it, but the weather would have made sure. And then that convenient dog walker had happened along with his helpful Labrador. Alison's previous mental health issues meant no-one was too surprised by her suicide. Certainly not enough to question it.

Caroline, Pete and I watched from the public gallery as the prosecution summed up their case. I held Caroline's hand as she sobbed silently, her daughter's callous disregard for the woman she perceived as standing between her and happiness, too hard to bear. I looked at Whittaker as he stood in the dock, wondering how my clever, warm-hearted friend had fallen for someone so utterly devoid of empathy.

As I'd predicted, once Whittaker realised things weren't looking good for him, he blamed everything on Beatrice, claiming that she'd become obsessed with him and he was too weak to resist. She had, he claimed, planned the whole thing and he, captivated by her, had got in too deep. However, challenged in a police interview, his anger flared up and he implicated himself, his arrogance and vanity so near the surface that it was easy to scratch.

I'd wanted to visit Bea on remand in prison before the trial, but I couldn't as I was going to be a witness for the prosecution. I had so many questions to ask, but I knew it was pointless because the main one was 'why?' and the answer was simply that she loved him. Even when faced with his back-pedalling as he tried to wriggle out of the charges against him, she refused to turn on him.

Seeing Bea found guilty of murder and conspiracy to commit murder was hard. The two life sentences, albeit running concurrently, meant that it would be many years before she was free.

"I'm sixty-four now. I'll probably be long gone before she's released," Caroline said beside me, almost under her breath. "I might never get to hug her again."

Bea looked across at us as the judge pronounced his sentence, and finally I saw the realisation of it all dawn on her. The consequences of letting herself fall for the wrong man, of not seeing him for what he was, of allowing him to trick her into sharing his monstrous way of thinking.

I had so many questions and couldn't shake the feeling that we'd all let Bea down after Liam died. If she'd been able to talk to someone she might not have withdrawn from the world and could have coped with the grief. She may have got over it and gone back to being the confident, out-going woman that she used to be.

But at that moment I dropped my eyes, unable to meet hers for fear of letting her see the turmoil of my own emotions. I'd lost my oldest friend and had to come to terms with the fact she'd done such terrible things.

PETE and I were quiet on the drive to Heathrow. I couldn't get away from the idea that that while we were on our way to Las Vegas for Jason's birthday celebrations, Bea was on her way to prison, facing at least twenty years behind bars. While we were partying, seeing the Grand Canyon from a helicopter, dining at the best restaurants and drinking the finest champagne, she would be settling into her cell and getting used to prison catering.

However, the sadness I felt at her, albeit justified, conviction, was balanced by the satisfaction of watching Jeremy Whittaker sentenced.

Giving my evidence was hard as I described how he'd tried to stab me and then run off down the street, still carrying that knife, able to do who knew what damage to another innocent party. Not so much the incident itself, the worst of it was knowing that although Beatrice had been upstairs, watching and listening to him threaten me, she'd done nothing to try and stop him.

Pete had to give evidence too, although he wasn't distressed, just annoyed. The wound to his leg healed fine. Just five stitches and barely a scar. The black eye only hung around for a week or so, but long enough that some of his former comrades saw it. I suspected they'd be teasing him for years about sustaining more injuries at the hands of a Brummie property developer than he picked up in Iraq.

As we drove, I tried to put it all out of my mind and concentrate on the next couple of weeks. My phone buzzed as a text arrived and I looked down at it, assuming it would be another missive from my mother about the trial and what was being reported in the papers.

My attention was sharpened though when I saw that in fact, the message was from a dealer in South Africa, who, at my request, had been quietly letting it be known he was looking for work by French Impressionists for a collector:

"Hello, Kate. About that Renoir you've been trying to trace. A young man came into my gallery today to tell me about a painting of his grandfather's that he wants to sell. He's happy to take a lower valuation for a quick, very discreet sale. Name of Julius Hoffman. I've told him I'll have to talk to my client and I'll be in touch. How soon can you get here?"

He'd attached a photo and I smiled; here was the Larssens' Renoir. From the moment we'd found the acid-splashed canvas, my instincts had told me that it was a fake. I was sure Hoffman was too venal to destroy something that valuable. I wouldn't let it escape me a second time.

"Hey, Pete. You know we have a few weeks off?"

"We do. I'm looking forward to it." He glanced across at me, hearing the excitement in my voice.

"Yeah, well, after Vegas, how about a trip to Cape Town? I need to see a man about a Renoir."

ACKNOWLEDGMENTS

Thanks to everyone who has advised, assessed and made suggestions for improving this manuscript. Special thanks must go to Jane Badger for her editorial input, Barry Hutchison for his publishing advice, and a mass of people who've dispensed advice in books, blog posts and emails about the workings of the art trade.

Also in no particular order, a massive thank you to Helen Barrell, Jacqueline Carrington Fallow, Martin Page, Sarah Painter, Alison Belsham, Jane Anderson, Marie and Dale Sheehan. Plus lots of people who I've probably missed off the list - please forgive me if that's you.

And of course, massive thanks to my husband, Malcolm, and son, Magnus, whose humour, encouragement and tea-making are always appreciated.

A FREE KATE CARPENTER BOOK WHEN YOU JOIN MY READERS CLUB

One of the things I love about writing is my contact with readers. Join my Readers Club and I'll let you know about forthcoming books and other news. You can also download a free Kate Carpenter story—Vanishing Point—as a welcome gift from me - find out how Kate met Pete in Belarus and what became of a stolen Van Gogh.

Just visit www.vanessarobertson.co.uk

Reviews are hugely appreciated by authors and they help readers find books they might enjoy. If you have enjoyed Trace Evidence and can spare a few minutes to leave a review, I'd be really grateful. Even a single sentence is helpful.

ALSO BY VANESSA ROBERTSON

Don't Blink

A stolen painting. A gangster intent on revenge. And nothing is what it seems.

Art consultant Kate Carpenter has an off-the-books sideline in art recovery, dealing with thieves, gangsters and the occasional war criminal to reunite priceless artworks with their owners. But when she refuses a request from the owner of one missing painting, Yuri Sokolov isn't prepared to take no for an answer.

Her knowledge has cost him millions, he wants revenge, and he isn't planning to show any mercy. The only way that Kate can get Yuri Sokolov to keep his distance is to find out exactly what happened to his painting, but when she starts scraping away at the surface, she finds that nothing is exactly as it appears.

Don't Blink is the first book in the Kate Carpenter series.

ALSO BY VANESSA ROBERTSON

Death Will Find Me

A former spy and her murdered husband.

Working in covert operations during World War One left Tessa with scars she still carries. Her hasty marriage is falling apart and after discovering her husband in a compromising position at a country house party, she tells him that she wants a divorce. But when James' body is found in a lonely stone bothy the next morning, Tessa is Inspector Hamish Rasmussen's only suspect.

Back in Edinburgh, links to another death force Rasmussen to enlist her help. Together they set off on a pursuit that once again brings Tessa face to face with the brutality of war and the desperate lengths that people will go to in order to protect those they love.

Will Tessa be able to prevent a final murder or will she become the killer's latest victim?

Printed in Great Britain
by Amazon

67792633R00158